ELAINE PASCALE

THE SOLSTICE

TREPIDATIO
PUBLISHING

ISBN: 978-1-68510-152-7 (tpb)
ISBN: 978-1-68510-153-4 (ebook)
The Library of Congress Cataloging-in-Publication data is available upon request.

First printing edition: April 11, 2025
Printed by Trepidatio Publishing in the United States of America.
Cover Artwork: Mikio Murakami
Edited by Sean Leonard
Proofreading, Cover Layout, & Interior Layout by Scarlett R. Algee

Trepidatio Publishing, an imprint of JournalStone Publishing
1400 North Wood Rd.
Murphysboro, IL 62966

Trepidatio books may be ordered through booksellers or by contacting:
JournalStone | www.journalstone.com

To Michael, for venturing through a dozen states to bring me to where I belong. To Christopher and Sierra for following. And to the swamps of Florida for providing the characters in this story.

THE SOLSTICE

Chapter 1
Bad Medicine

In this version of Hell, the woman in front of you will never stop arguing with the manager. The woman has privilege, clearly identified by both her age and the strap of color she wears around her neck. That is the only reason she is engaging in verbal combat. You know you have to wait patiently even though you are trying to purchase medication that requires refrigeration. The medicine has been sitting on a shelf and is growing warmer by the minute.

The manager is patiently trying to explain that they cannot take last-minute deli orders, especially with it being a holiday evening.

"I always order my charcuterie board here and I never have to give notice." She leans toward the manager and says in an indignant growl, "I may have to start taking my business elsewhere."

This is not Hell. It is the market on Solstice, which is a kind of hell for people like you.

You would have stayed home, had you not needed the medicine. Your food money had gone to the doctor who had written the prescription. As he handed it to you, he said, "You might wait until after tonight. You know, see if you need it." The doctor wore a red band on his neck.

You have tried ceasing medication before. You know you can't afford the monthly prescription, and you also fear that it will soon be unavailable. The Red Bands decide what medications to offer and to whom they can be offered. Eventually Solidox will be the only pharmaceutical on the market, and only for the Red Bands.

The Red Bands decide everything. Due to their experience on this earth, they feel they are best equipped to make determinations.

Without medicine, you blamed yourself for everything, including this new normal. While life had not been perfect, it had been mostly good for you. You had a family, you were educated, you had goals. Things had been fine, if not a little boring.

Like punching a bruise to see if it still hurt, you had wanted to revisit your true self. This meant stopping all chemicals. You had convinced yourself of false memories of a happier time, a freer time, when you had felt both ups and downs and had not operated on a sedated middle ground. You had forgotten that the ups and downs were not fun like a rollercoaster; they were scary like free-falling into an abyss.

In that abyss, you realized that you had too many belongings in your room. That stuff was holding you back. If you could only jettison some things, you would be lighter and able to be *up* again. You spent days in your room with the shades drawn, not sleeping, not eating, just looking at old memories and determining that everything was too important to throw out. Eventually, you resolved to dispose of an old diary because the cover had a stripe of yellow and yellow brings complications.

After the trash collection had come, you remembered that you could not simply throw things out because there was no way to predict how different life would be without that item.

You hadn't come close to predicting the new normal.

After the diary had been discarded, the storm had come. The storm had brought the new rules. The things you had enjoyed were no longer available. You were forced out of your home to struggle on your own. Every minute felt like a struggle. Even on medication, there were no more ups; the world ran on a low frequency.

Then the Red Bands instituted the Solstices.

You have learned that without the medication you become suicidal. You begin to wonder if that might be a preferable state in this world. It might be better to kill yourself, to take control of your narrative, as opposed to participating in the Solstice. Something keeps you going, and that something moved you to go to the market.

A sneeze is cloying at your nose. You try to stifle it; you never want to seem weak or sick. Moreover, you never want to draw attention to yourself. Those that fly under the radar live the longest. But sneezes have minds of their own, and it escapes, causing the Red Band to turn her attention to you. The woman eyes you appraisingly and then runs her tongue over her parched and wrinkled lips. Her shirt reads, *Boat Hair; Don't Care*, even though her platinum hair is perfectly coifed. You remember the days before the mandatory Solstice celebrations when those types of shirts made women of a certain age seem part of a clique. The neck bands now establish order, and the old woman seems displeased when she sees yours is a shade of lavender.

"Ma'am?" The manager retrieves a booklet of savings stamps from beneath the register. The stamps could easily feed an entire family for three months. You look at the medicine in your hand. It is all you can afford this trip. You wish you had some stamps to buy food. The Red Bands have no need for the stamps, but the woman snatches them greedily.

"And remember...tonight..." The manager winks and straightens his green band.

When it is your turn, you begin counting your stamps and the manager interrupts to ask for your ID.

You motion toward your neck band: you are an adult. He responds by pointing to a sign behind his shoulder. The sign is written in cursive. In the days of the Solstice, all signs are written in cursive. The sign is difficult to decipher, but it says something about requiring appropriate health insurance vouchers for medication along with proof of proper employment.

You sigh. "They don't let us have proper employment; you know that."

The manager raises an eyebrow. "Maybe your husband?"

The rules had changed so rapidly that no action had been taken to stop them. The rules had also been subtly approved outside of the realm of social media. People who now wear the lavender and blue bands had been unfamiliar with the types of communication that had been used. And if they happened to be aware of them, they were uninterested.

"I don't..." You start to explain but then realize that the Red Band rules allow for no excuses. Things change so often and with such vague parameters that there is no room for refutation. You continue counting stamps, adding a few extra for the manager's trouble in having to deal with someone in a lavender band.

He rolls his eyes at your paltry bribe but accepts it anyway. "We take personal checks, you know."

The manager is being spiteful. He knows that lavender bands are not allowed bank accounts and that it will be decades until you can wear the green let alone the red band. If you live that long.

You clutch the medicine bag tightly and head for home. In your head, you constantly calculate how life would be different if you had been allowed your inheritance. You would have enough stamps for food, and you might have even been able to pay for protection from the Solstice celebration. Your parents had been victims of the Solstice, and the goods of the victims are plundered by the victors. They had been early victims, so your parents had still been allowed to own a house, and a car, and have a savings account. Someone in a red band now enjoyed those possessions.

Your parents had been Green Bands. They were the generation that would become Red Bands the soonest if allowed to live; wearing a green band was basically like wearing a bullseye. You had worried about them, and when not taking medication your anxiety had reached panic levels. On the day of the first Solstice, you had not had the opportunity to tell your parents you loved them. When each of you survived that event, you determined that not saying those words had protected them. You continued to not say the words and your parents continued to survive. Until they didn't. The only honorarium of their death you received was a bouquet of roses, because the Red Bands value roses.

Roses can be cut and possessed. The purpose of a bouquet is to watch it die. This fits the Red Bands' *raison d'être*: to collect things that have no practical use.

They also love to gather resources. They gather properties. They hoard necessities. They waste and discard food as if it were a hobby. The Red Bands suck the rings from the fingers of their victims as they devour the flesh around the jewelry.

They love the act of gathering so much that the Solstice celebrations were crafted and created for this purpose. Prior to the celebrations, the Red Bands had been forced to hunt. But hunting proved dangerous. At best, the Red Bands ended up with defensive scratches and teeth marks. At worst, they didn't survive the event. It was determined that hunting was far less profitable than being able to pluck victims from the street.

Back at your room in the Lavender living quarters, you swallow the medicine to spite the doctor. You have every intention of living through the night. The medicine is bitter and leaves a bad taste in your mouth, but your entire existence is one of battling lingering acrimony.

The sky is darkening quickly, which is why the winter Solstice is favored. The joke is that the action taking place can coincide with the "early bird specials." The joke is only funny to those wearing red bands.

The announcement is made over the only television station on the island. The station airs mostly the news. Occasionally they broadcast shows from the past in which one person sues another and a judge makes the ultimate decision on who wins the court cases. The Red Bands relate to the judges, and they respect quick, humorless verdicts.

The announcement comes as no surprise, as everyone has been preparing for the Solstice. The Red Bands prepare as if it were a celebration. For everyone else, it mimics the daily fight for survival, only to the extreme.

The announcement is the prelude for the forced evacuations. Everyone must leave their homes and go to the streets. Doors must be left open. Anyone found inside will be shot on sight.

As you have been trained to do at Solstice, you turn off the television and get ready to leave. You are allowed to wear dark clothing, but your lavender neck band must be visible. The lucky will live to see morning; the unlucky will be tranquilized and then preyed upon while immobile. No one wants to witness a devouring; it is enough to simply imagine it.

You pocket your keys even though the door must remain unlocked. If a search is warranted, the Red Bands must be able to enter freely. The keys are all you carry. The Red Bands hate cell phones and refuse to repair the towers that had been destroyed in the storm. Only land lines are in working order, and only certain people are allowed telephones.

You feel dizzy as you pass through your open doorway. You are experiencing heart palpitations that are stronger than the fear-based ones you normally feel during this ritual. You are sweating and your throat aches with dryness. You cannot afford to go back in for a drink; it would appear as if you were not obeying the rules, and the judge-loving Red Bands manage the disobedient with swiftness and cruelty.

The air is crisp and cool, yet you are damp with a sickly warmth. You stumble down the front steps and nearly collide with the others who are making their way onto the street. No one is allowed to hide, but movement is permitted. Some Red Bands have poor peripheral vision, and some are lousy shots with the tranquilizer guns. Walking in a zigzag pattern has been a strategy incorporated by many.

Numerous Lavender Bands are moving in quick, short spurts. Their rate is sporadic and unpredictable. No one wants to stand too close to anyone else; being collateral damage is not a noble way to go. Neither is being eaten alive, but no Lavender Band has control over that.

A woman wearing a green band has found her way into your neighborhood. This tactic has been incorporated in the past, as Green Bands feel the Lavenders are safe. The Lavenders are ripening, aging like a fine wine. This woman may not even realize where she is. She is crying. She is limping and muttering to herself between sobs. You can hear her saying, "Right...now right...right," as she drags her hobbled foot into position. Between her slow gait and her green band, she is not likely to make it through the night.

Despite being years younger than the limping woman, you are not moving much better than she is. Your body has grown heavy. It had started in your shoulders and then moved to your hips until you felt as if your body were separating at the torso. You can still hear, "Right...right...now right," and you wonder how you have not been able to move farther away from this nearly stationary woman. You lean forward, trying to propel yourself onward. You stumble, which is good, as it makes you a challenging target.

You amble as if drunk and your insides feel warm with an uncomfortable intoxication. Your head is pounding, and the thirst has intensified. You want nothing more than to go back inside and collapse onto your bed. That action would be a death warrant, and for a reason you cannot explain, you still desire to remain alive.

Your legs begin to feel as if they are very far away. Maybe they have gone back to your bed on their own, leaving the rest of you to fend for yourself. A part of you realizes that idea is ridiculous, and it makes you smile as you picture your legs tucked beneath your comforter, sleeping as if they did not have a care in the world.

You push forward again but are barely able to make any ground. Your gait slows until you clumsily bend at the knees and fall onto your side.

It is hard to breathe on your side, but you no longer have the strength to roll over onto your back. Some grass tickles your nose, but you cannot push it away.

The neighborhood looks different from this angle. The residences appear thinner, as if they lost substance when their inhabitants left. A few pairs of feet move by you. Some are zigzagging. Those feet wear sneakers, and the laces are in double-knots. No one can afford to trip or to stop to retie a shoe.

Two pairs of feet in the distance are not moving quickly. One pair of feet are in boat shoes, the other in sparkly sandals. The feet are walking directly toward you.

Hands are placed under your armpits, yet those hands feel like they are miles away. One set of hands has long nails that bite into your skin. The pain is not so bad, but you know it will get worse. You are dragged a short distance and then placed on the back bench of a golf cart.

"You timed that perfectly," a woman says, sliding into the passenger seat in front of you. She turns to look at you, smacking her red lips. It is the woman from the market. She is no longer wearing her *Boat Hair* shirt. She has on a sparkly sequined blouse that catches the streetlights and makes your eyes hurt to look at it.

"To be fair, I warned her to wait and take it tomorrow. But you know how they are." The man behind the steering wheel laughs. It is your doctor, the one who gave you the medicine. You curse yourself for trusting a Red Band, especially on the day of the Solstice celebration.

"She is utterly useless, isn't she?" The woman grins and plays with the rings that she has stacked on her fingers. Her bracelets make clicking noises as she moves.

"They all are. Can barely fend for themselves. We are basically doing them a favor..."

You lose track of time until the golf cart goes over a few bumps that you recognize as being the speed breakers that are near Rodeo where the Red Bands reside. Rodeo was named after the section of Beverly Hills where shopping was luxurious. The Red Bands like reminders of extravagance; they believe they manifest lavishness by repeatedly conjuring its image.

Rodeo is packed to near-hoarder proportions with the belongings of those who have succumbed to prior Solstices.

"They are not only useless, but greedy too." The woman toys with her diamond necklace. "Like babies, just wanting their needs met. Needing frivolous things like their avocado toast and streaming movie subscriptions. The power outage really showed them. They had no idea how to entertain themselves without the internet."

The doctor places a gentle hand on her knee. He is not the most competent of one-handed drivers and the cart sways, causing you to slide around on the slim bench that holds you aloft. "It was so nice when we went back to the old ways. The stamp books were bittersweet. I remember my mother collecting the stamps. I used to help her put them in the books they gave us."

She nods. "And then we got to pick something out with the stamps. What a fun time!"

"These...*others*... They really have no idea how to save for what they want. Everything was automatic for them—just the swipe of a card and more debt. But you were right." He pats her knee again. "We act as stewards for them now. It's better."

"They are so fragile." She reaches around and pinches your skin. Her nails are long and manicured. From what you had seen when you were on the ground, her toenails match in color but not length. Even in the colder weather, the Red Band women wear open-toed shoes, protecting themselves from the elements by wearing nylons or transparent compression socks inside of them. "We survived with no seatbelts, no bicycle helmets."

"And when things started to get tough for us, we took charge."

She laughs. "We know how to age with grace!"

"We are the greatest generation!"

"I thought that was our parents?"

"Okay, the *final* generation!"

The woman laughs again and peers at you in the back seat. You are barely on the small bench and have no way of righting yourself.

"Let's go to the pond," she suggests. "It's so romantic."

He shrugs and turns the wheel sharply, almost causing you to fly out of the vehicle. You wish you were able to fly out of the vehicle. "We got any appetizers?"

She grunts. "That stupid manager wouldn't allow me to place the order for the charcuterie board."

"Bastard." He turns the wheel again and then slows to a stop. "He knows we always have a charcuterie board."

"He was being obstinate. I can't believe the audacity."

"We can swing by the Green Band quarters and take care of him later. He's too...*fluffy* to wander too far in the night."

They open a bottle of champagne and fill two flutes.

"Either way, tonight, we feast."

"Don't we always?" She pulls open her oversized purse which rivals her blouse in sheer shininess. She has a metal container from which she removes a pill. She puts the pill on her tongue and grimaces. You shudder, knowing she is taking her Solidox. "Down the hatch."

The doctor digs in his shirt pocket and removes a pill that he takes with a large swig of champagne. "It won't be long at all," he says and turns on a small radio. The song "Precious and Few" by Climax begins to play.

"Awww," the woman says and squeezes the doctor's hand.

He grimaces and grasps at his abdomen. Then he leans back and looks up at the sky. "A beautiful night."

"Isn't it always?" She sighs. "Solstice is the most glorious time. The grandest time." She digs in her purse again and pulls out a steak knife, tongs, and a melon baller. She examines each before laying them on her lap. "How do you want to start?"

He glances at the tools. "Melon baller. You know I'm a sucker for eyes."

"That's the difference between us. I always save the best for last. Delayed gratification."

He nods. "That is a good strategy as well. I could learn to show some restraint."

She giggles and puts her hand in his lap. "Let's not become too restrained now. It'll spoil all the fun."

Bile rises in your throat. This was something you hadn't considered: Would they be having sex over your corpse? *With* your corpse?

She inhales deeply. Her nostrils pull back for another inhale and she frowns. "That's not right."

"What isn't?"

She turns her head toward you and sniffs. "It should smell like beef au jus, and macaroni and cheese, and peach pie. You know, like comfort food."

"And goodnight kisses," the doctor mumbles.

"What?" When he doesn't answer her, she shoves his shoulder and points to you in the back seat.

He leans over and takes a long whiff. "You're right."

"What did you put in her medication?"

"Exactly what I was supposed to put in it."

She taps the steak knife with her long fingernails. "Something went wrong."

"This was a new tweak. It was supposed to be...*new*."

"It's not working."

He becomes indignant. "I'm the one who invented it; nothing ever goes wrong."

"It did now. And we have wasted half the night on this...this..."

"Shit." He rubs his forehead and suddenly looks very tired. "I think...maybe it got warm. The medicine, I mean. It might have gotten warm."

"What happens when it gets warm?"

He nods in your direction. "This. Smells...useless...completely fucking useless."

"Did you tell the idiot manager to keep it refrigerated?"

The doctor looks to the sky, thinking.

The woman crosses her arms. "Oh my God. What do we do now?"

The doctor turns his wrist so he can see his watch. "There's time. You brought the darts, right?"

"Of course, but the good ones will be taken by this point."

"We don't know that. We gotta hope for the best." He playfully chucks her chin. "That's what we do, right? Hope for the best."

She nods and rights herself in her seat.

You are shocked as they turn the ignition back on and begin to drive. You had thought that the pond would be the place where you died. You had been sad about that, as you still want more life even if that meant more of this.

They both complain of hunger as they drive back over the speed bumps and travel from the roads that are well kept to the ones that are mostly neglected.

They drop you onto the sidewalk in front of your apartment, which is more than you could have hoped for. The sidewalk is cold and hard, but you are safe, as your medicine is causing a reverse effect on the Solidox. You don't believe you smell any different, but you are not a Red Band. You are thrilled with your repulsive odor, and you begin to wonder if rolling in shit might be a new Solstice strategy.

The couple pauses and looks you over one last time. The woman leans out of the cart and smiles at you. "Next time," she promises.

Chapter 2
The Market

Climax was singing about moments being "precious and few" as Leroy clocked in for the day. As manager, he did not need to perform this action as he oversaw payroll, but he did so out of habit. The song, which was replayed in the store three times over the course of eighteen hours, reminded him of his parents, as they had loved it. There was some connection to a prom or dance that crafted nostalgia around it, but he hadn't actually listened when they had spoken about it.

He put his lunch in the break-room refrigerator. He had written his name on the Tupperware. This was not to distinguish it from other lunches. He marked it because there were so few containers. He was one of the rare workers who could afford to bring a lunch to eat during the break and he didn't want it stolen. There were plenty of cameras in the store, including in the break room, but desperation might make someone ignore the potential of being caught.

He had packed a scrapple sandwich and Jell-O salad. It was what he had eaten growing up because it was what his father had eaten growing up. His father had been a stickler for tradition. The man had resisted change with a warlike quality because "change was always for the worse." As his father aged, he openly criticized each and every political, social, and technological advancement. If only his father could see the way things were run now.

It was Solstice, and Leroy wished he had the luxury of staying home. It was difficult to face the Red Bands while they prepared. But someone had to make sure the kerosene tanks were full and ready to rent for cookouts. Someone had to field the complaints about the products that had been there since the hurricane and would not be replaced once sold. Someone had to maintain the semblance of normalcy that the Red Bands demanded. In this world, he was that someone.

After making sure the cashiers were opening the registers, Leroy began to put together the charcuterie board orders for the deli. What the Red Bands consider charcuterie was basically sliced meats. With the majority of the farmland decimated, and no bridge for trucks to pass over, inventory had become a creative endeavor. He had been forced to scavenge the leftovers from the Solstice. There were times when he held his own "celebration"—no one noticed if a random Blue or Lavender Band went missing. He was not worried about punishment for these activities. If the Red Bands knew of the ethics involved, they probably would not care or would chalk it up to necessary population control.

Each day when Elton John bid goodbye to the Yellow Brick Road, Leroy made his way to the back office. The irony of the Red Bands selecting that song for the rotation was not lost on him. Recently, he had begun practicing pulling his chin above the bar he had installed in the doorframe in the back of the manager's office. He was pleased with the progress he was making; he was able to clear the bar at least five times. Sometimes, he was able to wiggle and struggle until his shoulders ran parallel with the frame. That was his goal: to have the strength to leverage his weighty body aloft.

He was able to watch the stock clerks move canned goods as he exercised. They moved the same cans from one shelf to the next, as no new products could be brought onto the island.

The clerks usually gave him a good ribbing when he exercised, and this day was no different.

"Work on that gut, man. You're looking like a snack, and not in a good way," Herb muttered as he climbed onto the rickety shelving to reach some cans. Worker's comp was a thing of the past, but workers were willing to take the risk. Dying on the job was preferable to dying during Solstice.

Herb had no right to talk. All employees were part of the Green Band population. They were feeble and tired. Most had sallow, saggy skin. None of them looked terribly appetizing, but the Solidox pills the

Red Bands consumed took care of that. Because Leroy managed the store, and because he was in charge of inventory, he was one of the few able to sport a belly paunch.

In the Green Band housing where Leroy lived, people stuck to themselves. He did not have to hide the fact that he brought home the iced-over frozen products, the dented cans, and the past-expiration-date dairy. The Red Bands wanted those items discarded, but he had never been caught. He had a theory that the Red Bands had a waste kink simply to spite their Great Depression-era elders. The Red Bands had been raised with strict edicts to ration and were still rebelling against that. Years before the rules changed, when the Red Bands had been called "Boomers," Leroy and the employees had complained about the weird ways of that generation. Leroy had repeatedly said that the Boomers were "hard to stomach." It wasn't purely a cliché; he had suffered stomach ulcers putting up with customers from that particular age bracket. It chilled him to think back on his prior cavalier attitude, knowing what the Red Bands now put in *their* stomachs.

Leroy was outside hosing off the sidewalk when he heard Jim Croce's voice coming from inside the store. Croce wanted to save time in a bottle, which was an attractive idea. The Red Bands would consider it hoarding if anyone wearing any other hue managed to save anything. The Red Bands were waging their own war against time and winning. They had no need for bottles, only for Solidox.

He glanced at the burger joint down the street. A Green Band was struggling to hold a platter aloft while roller-skating to the vehicle that awaited her in the parking lot. Green Bands did not have the balance they once did, and they were not privy to Solidox to help them with their comorbidities. They tended to be weaker as a group, but the Red Bands did not trust the Blue Bands and they trusted the Lavender Bands even less, so the Green Bands were employed to do their bidding.

This particular Green Band was also new to the job and probably had not been on skates in decades. Leroy hadn't seen the prior waitress since the last Solstice. He could confidently guess what had happened to her.

The parking lot of the burger place was nearly full. The Red Bands were out and about and consuming as they normally did. After the Solstice they will rest. Their stomachs will be full, yet they will still hunger for control.

Leroy suspected that the nostalgic burger place copied his method for acquiring meat. There hadn't been a lot of stray animals after the storm, but there had been plenty of misplaced people.

Leroy noticed movement from across the street. It was the woman he has been secretly calling "Holly Blue" after the beautiful butterfly of the same name. He felt he was being extra clever in tying her hidden nickname into the color of band she wore. She rarely came into the store; purchases were few and far between for anyone who wasn't a Red Band. When she did come in, he would say the same joke: that she should apply for a job since she would have no commute. She would always point to her blue band in answer. She wouldn't be employable until she lived long enough to swap out for a green band. Unlike the name Holly Blue, the mention of a commute was not a clever statement. Since the bridge had been destroyed, no one commuted.

Placing the Blue Bands close to the island businesses had been a strategic move. It forced the Green Bands to engage in a bit of travel to get to their jobs and forced the Blue Bands to have in their view entitlements they could not have. While Green Band salaries were slim, they were salaries. Some of Leroy's coworkers thought that the Blue Bands kept tabs on them. The Blue Bands knew those in green were heavily targeted on Solstice and eventually there would be job vacancies that would need to be filled.

Holly Blue saw him looking and gave a polite wave. He waved back. It was hard in this world to develop rapport with anyone, and even harder to want to. If he lived long enough, he might have the luxury of having a relationship with someone. The basic needs of the Red Bands were met, so they could invest in hobbies and social obligations. They were almost like the adolescents of old in terms of their lack of responsibility.

Croce was replaced by Mama Cass. She was hoping her lover would dream a little dream of her. Leroy sometimes found himself dreaming about Holly Blue while he was awake. He would imagine that she came into the store when he was the only one there. They would talk and laugh and be important to each other. He hadn't been important to anyone since his parents died, nor had he had anyone he particularly cared for.

Love was far too risky in the days of the Solstice.

Brooklyn Bridge was singing about the worst thing that could happen. Leroy was envious of that voice singing about heartbreak as if it were the foulest thing a person could face. There were two things that tied with being "the worst" in Leroy's life. One was the idea of being consumed without consent. The other was the Red Band customers. The customer standing in front of Leroy was a connoisseur of delivering psychic pain. She was a regular. He had seen her *Boat Hair; Don't Care* shirt more times than he could count, and he always thought that she seemed like the last person to have that as her motto. She was complaining about not having a charcuterie platter. He probably could have scrounged up enough ingredients to make her one, but he knew it would be met with additional complaints and derision, and denying her what she wanted made him feel good. She threatened to take her business elsewhere; an empty threat, as there really was no "elsewhere." He offered her stamps for her troubles. The stamps and asking for her to remember him later were for optics only. He had no intention of participating in the Solstice, so he did not need her mercy.

What he was planning was a gamble. If caught hiding, he faced a gang-style execution. If caught on the street, he became someone's dinner. As store manager, he was replaceable. His role offered him no security from the Solstice. He had decided that he wanted to be the architect of his own security system. He also decided he would rather die suddenly than be consumed. And if all went well, he would not have to endure either.

The Red Bands didn't touch the executed; they didn't want meat after it was dead. He wasn't sure if the Solidox failed to work on cold meat or if they simply had enough prey available that they could afford to be picky. The Red Bands rarely felt that they had enough of anything, so Leroy assumed it was the former.

He watched the *Boat Hair* woman stomp off, clutching her stamps that she would most likely never use. The next customer was a young woman, attempting to buy medicine. Leroy could predict that this exchange would not go well either. The Lavender Bands never have enough stamps to purchase what they want; that is part of the Red Band's policy. He asked for ID, hoping to get the woman's name, promising himself that if his plan works, he will try to help others. It was nearly impossible to not be selfish in a world with regular Solstices, but Leroy was willing to try altruism as a cure for loneliness.

The woman was not having it. She motioned toward her neck band. She wanted the transaction to be over as soon as possible. Leroy understood that, yet he found himself growing irritated. The Red Bands tended to leave the younger offerings alone at Solstice. This woman had less to worry about than he did. He pointed to a sign behind his shoulder, wanting to watch her squint as she tried to make out the cursive. All Lavender Bands struggled with that sign. The sign itself was another form of optics; managers no longer cared about proper insurance as there was no oversight remaining regarding the few medicines still in existence. Leroy decided to reserve his charitable feelings for Holly Blue.

The medicine buyer sighed. "They don't let us have proper employment; you know that," she said.

Leroy was well aware of that rule. He oversaw hiring at the store and he knew of the consequences of employing anyone below a green band. He toyed with the woman a bit, asking about her husband and reminding her of bank policies before accepting the meager stamps she had offered. She had insulted him further with a paltry bribe, which he almost shoved back at her before deciding to keep it. Had she shown her ID, had she made any attempt to be more than a nameless customer to him, the entire transaction would have gone differently.

Billy Joel began singing about honesty being hard to find and Leroy shifted his anger from the customer to Mr. Joel. He refused to feel any guilt over his plan. Others would do the same in his shoes. In a world with Solstices, honesty got you killed.

The store must close promptly on Solstice. Leroy had no issue complying with that rule; in fact, he wanted to close early so he could begin to enact his plan. He knew that any change to the regular schedule would draw unwanted attention, so he tapped his foot eagerly to the music that he had heard too many times but hoped he would live to hear again.

Behind locked doors, he disabled the cameras, even though he was the only one who would ever be asked to review the security tapes. Normally, he would exit out the back, pulling the large security door shut. This time, he went to the back, lifted the sliding door, and then slammed it shut again. He hoped that if anyone were listening, they would believe he had left. It was too dark to see, so that audio confirmation would have to suffice.

He knew he was being paranoid. The Red Bands did not lurk around waiting pre-Solstice. They engaged in celebration, in revelry. They drank champagne and took their Solidox and feasted. Once everyone was forced to evacuate their homes, the Red Bands used their darts and then simply plucked the meal they desired.

Elvis crooned that it was now or never. "You got that right," Leroy whispered. If anyone were to check his home, they would find it empty, per the rules. If anyone checked the store, they would find it empty as well. He slid a panel in the ceiling above the snack aisle aside and pulled himself up. The chin-ups paid off.

The space in the ceiling was large enough for him to lay comfortably, but it was claustrophobic. Yet, it was far less frightening than being on the street awaiting attack. There was movement and energy in his space which he attributed to rats, and there were smells that were not noticeable from the store below. It was too dark for him to see, and the music had shut off for the night. He hoped he might fall asleep and wake up when Solstice was over.

He wondered why he hadn't thought of this before. He had been in denial about the Solstices for too long. Originally, he had faith that someone would put a stop to them, but that faith had dwindled. He began to talk himself through the store's music playlist in the order they are played as a way of quieting his mind and, eventually, he drifted off.

A scream woke him. He tried to sit up but quickly remembered that he was in a confined space. There were footsteps moving outside the store. People were running. Leroy held his breath, fearing they would try to enter the store, but it was locked up with steel shutters over the windows that prevented invasion from the hungry on non-Solstice nights.

More screams could be heard along with a loud thud. A voice yelled "Help," and he recognized it. It was Holly Blue. His heart began to race. His first instinct was to feel around for a weapon. He could protect her; he could save her. He could be important to her, and she could be important to him. His second instinct, nearly following the first, was to close his eyes tightly and try to regulate his breathing.

The screams grew louder and were accompanied by sounds of pummeling. He knew that meant the Red Bands were tenderizing their meat. A customer once brought back some steak, complaining that meat that was not terrified lacked flavor. Said steak had come from a body executed during the Solstice and Leroy wanted to correct the customer, but there was no room for truth in his world. As the sound continued, Leroy tried very hard to not imagine what Holly Blue was experiencing. She was being tortured, she was being terrorized, and he was helpless to do anything about it. Selfishly, he lamented that he would no longer be able to wave at her from across the street or tell her his bad jokes.

The screams had an unearthly quality, as if the mind and throat and lungs were completely separate and the voice would carry on indefinitely. He had thought the paralysis would make it impossible to scream, but he had been wrong. There were sobs mixed in and pleas that were unbearable to hear. Leroy started going through the individual song lyrics in the store's rotation. He began with the Climax song, which repeated midday and in the late evening, and then moved to the Carpenters and then Freda Payne. By the time he got to Croce, the screams subsided.

Eventually, he was able to return to sleep, waking to the sound of Climax repeating their assertion that moments are precious and few. He stretched and smiled, realizing that he had made it and also that he did like the song.

Chapter 3
Goodnight Kisses

It had started with the cats.

> *Solidox, a tetracyclic antidepressant, has been proven to be a resourceful appetite stimulant in cats that suffer from chronic kidney disease (CKD) and certain cancers. By serving as an antagonist of histamine and serotonin receptors, Solidox plays a role in nausea suppression and vomit control, allowing the imbiber to swallow and digest proteins that might otherwise be found to be repellant.*

"Remember, you pretend to be asleep if we come back here." His mom glanced at him, more so at his reflection in the mirror, as she dragged a line of blush along her cheekbones. He always watched as she got ready for dates, it was one of the only times he was allowed in her room.

"Did you feed Shadow and the others?" she asked with concern. She didn't bother to ask if he had had any dinner. She hadn't bothered to check the cupboard or the fridge to see if there was anything he could make for himself. There had been one egg and some bread that still had spots without mold on it that he had been able to salvage. The pantry shelf that belonged to the cats was always stocked. She never seemed to forget to provide for them.

He hoped her date would go well. He believed that if she fell in love and got married, she would spend more time at home, and they would be a family. He was often in the apartment alone, with just the cats. John was only eight and had few friends and no means of visiting them, so he had to make do with the cats.

And, like their owner, his mother's cats were not friendly by nature.

"If we don't come back here and are gone very late, you will be fine. Just go to bed like a good boy."

"What about a goodnight kiss?"

"I can give you a kiss when you are asleep. It's just as good, right?"

He nodded. "Do you think... Do you love him, Momma?"

She snorted. "I don't believe in love any longer."

He took a deep breath. "I love you, so I believe in love."

She smiled, more at herself in the mirror than at him. "That's sweet."

He waited for her to reciprocate with a declaration of love, but she simply applied more mascara.

"And then when you do come home, we're going to go to the park, right? You promised."

She put down her make-up brush and looked at him directly this time. Her earrings glittered and he loved the way they sparkled beside her powdered skin. "I don't remember promising anything, but we will hope for the best." She smiled and gave him a playful chuck under his chin. "That's what we do, right? Hope for the best."

> The cats met inclusion criteria for the study if they had been diagnosed with CKD or cancer of the liver and were underweight/suffering from malnutrition. Cats were excluded if they had been provided with intravenous fluids during treatments.

By the time he was fourteen, John's mother began spending days at a time on her dates. None of the men became his father; he never even met most of them. He still socialized primarily with the cats as he had even fewer friends than he had in elementary school. As they aged, the other children began to smell the abandonment on him like a cheap perfume, and it made them want to avoid any contact. The cats' want for attention came sporadically, thus he passed the time by reading. He believed that if he were smart, his mother would be proud of him. As it stood, the only pride she felt was in his care of her cats.

There were six felines that lived in their small apartment. John was in charge of feeding them and cleaning the litter boxes. He was also expected to play with them and provide them with affection. He did not know much about feline enrichment, so he simply read aloud from his books, which seemed to intrigue a few of them. There was a Russian Blue called Ollie that would settle in John's lap when he opened a book, and he took a great liking to that cat.

The limitations of the study include that the cats were all domesticated. They had a history of medical attention. Some were provided special diets, and some were fed homemade food or table scraps. It is not known if Solidox would have an equal effect on feral cats who procure their own sustenance and are at risk for tapeworms and other digestive parasites.

Shadow, the Maine Coon, had become thinner. His ribs were noticeable from a distance, and his face had grown gaunt, showcasing sharp bones around his eye sockets. Sometimes the cat drooled a bit, but he had no appetite when offered food.

"I ask so little of you, only that you take care of the cats," his mother lamented one of the few times she was home.

"I do," he insisted.

"Then why does Shadow look like that? He was always such a handsome cat." When she purred out the word *handsome,* John realized that she had never called him that.

"How old is Shadow?"

She thought for a moment. "Your dad gave him to me. We had been on a date to a dance, and he surprised me with a kitten. I'm thinking he is fifteen or sixteen." He wondered if she knew how old he was. She never made much of his birthdays.

"I think he is just old, Momma."

Her face took on an even harder look than before. "He is *not* old. Cats can live for a very long time. Especially if they are well taken care of and loved. Apparently, he is not well taken care of, and it seems that only I love him."

"I...I love him...and I promise to do better, Momma." He hated when she was disappointed in him and would do anything to gain her approval.

"Well, John, I'm hoping for the best. That's what I always do." She swung her purse strap over her shoulder and made for the door, neglecting his goodnight kiss as usual.

Delimitations included that only the breeds of Persian, Maine Coon, Abyssinians, and Russian Blue were tested. The delimitation was made due to the size of the cats for ease of examinations, and similar life expectancy. Persians, Maine Coons, and Abyssinians are also known for a prevalence of kidney defects, making them useful for the purpose of the study.

As John cleaned up yet another puddle of Shadow's urine, he noted that the cat was somehow even thinner. At this rate, the cat would simply disappear without intervention. He was amazed that an animal could survive for so long looking like nothing more than skin and bones.

John had several medical books that his mother had picked up for him at church fundraisers. While she was lax about supplying him with food, she never hesitated to acquire books for him, especially those of the scholarly variety. This was partially because the books kept him quiet and entertained and partially because she had stopped believing she would ever be able to find a "wallet" that could satisfy her cravings for the good life. The men in her social circle, those that she attracted, were similarly patterned: under-educated and lacking motivation. She seemed to decide that her son could become her benefactor, so she encouraged any and all study on his part.

He took to the books ravenously. What his home lacked in nutritional offerings, it made up for in cerebral feedings. John was particularly interested in medicine; in finding ways to impede the natural process. He noticed how tired his mother appeared, how it took more make-up to brighten her face than it used to. As much as she was no help to him in terms of his basic needs, he did love her, and he feared her growing old.

And now there was Shadow, the eldest of the cats and failing in health at a frightening rate. John poured through his books, diagnosing chronic kidney disease in the feline, and seeking a way to reverse the symptoms. He kept several journals, detailing what the cat ate and what he refused. He noted the amount of water the cat consumed. He jotted down the frequency of urination and its appearance and odor. He weighed the cat on the kitchen scale and kept track of its heart rate.

If he could cure the cat, his mother would be so proud. She might even grow to love him.

Tumor type and size were recorded prior to beginning the treatment protocol.

One morning, when John's mother was still on a date from the previous evening, Shadow collapsed while trying to walk to his water bowl. John scooped the cat in his arms, his heart sinking at how light the cat now was. There had been a time when John had to support the cat with both arms, resting the feline's weight against his abdomen, struggling to lift the cat any higher. Now, he was easily able to lift the cat with one hand. Yet, he still used both arms, cradling the limp body as he tried to supply Shadow with water through an eye dropper.

Shadow's eyes rolled back, and he turned away from the water. John knew that without extreme intervention, the cat would die soon. The loose flesh told tales of dehydration, as did the sunken eyes that had once been so bright and round.

John took the cat to the sink, hoping to get some water into its mouth, and if that didn't work, he would rig an intravenous contraption from the needles his mother kept for sewing projects that were only spools of thread and procrastination.

His mother returned just in time to see John holding the lifeless cat in one hand, a bloodied needle in the other.

Tumors were smaller (≤.5 cm) and 12 out of 20 cats (60%) showed weight gain within the first 14 days of treatment. Solidox appears to be safe and well tolerated by the population of the study.

"I have no choice," his mother said sternly as she watched him packing his bags.

"I don't want to go," he managed between tears. He wanted to stay with her, in the only home he knew. There was mental comfort about the apartment in that he knew what to expect, even if there was little physical comfort.

"John, I saw what you were doing to that cat. You are..." She looked away and sighed. "I am afraid for my safety, having you in this house."

"But...I was trying to..."

"You can tell that story as many times as you like; it doesn't make it true."

The Russian Blue rubbed against his legs as John sat on his bed. When he bent to pet it, his mother recoiled.

"I don't think I want you touching them anymore."

John sniffed, refusing to let her see any further tears. He felt that if he behaved stoically, if he behaved like a grown man, then she would be proud of him. "How...how can you afford this school?"

She glanced to the door where a new fur coat was hanging. Her entire wardrobe had recently been upgraded. "A friend is helping me."

"I was trying to cure him, Shadow," John insisted, but his mother wouldn't listen. "I don't want to go away," he repeated numerous times to deaf ears.

At the train station, she chucked him playfully beneath his chin. "We are going to hope for the best, right? That's what we do."

Per custom, she did not kiss him goodbye.

Solidox is unparalleled as an appetite stimulant.

While in school, his mother moved and failed to disclose her new address.

The school kept him fed, kept his uniform clean, and in that sense did more parenting than his mother ever had. He thrived while studying and earned the respect of the other students, who were impressed by his drive and mental prowess. The dormitory even had a resident cat that he befriended and shared parts of his meal with.

After John's eighteenth birthday, his mother cut off all communication, verifying that she was aware of his date of birth.

> *Even food items containing mold appeared appetizing after a dose of Solidox, where prior to the dose the moldy foods were avoided. It also appeared that scents were masked, nearly transformed. The cats could be provided the strongest-smelling agents after dosage and still want to eat. In subsequent trials, food was soaked in vinegar; then laced with cloves; then dusted with a mix of cumin, garlic, and ginger, and the cats approached the offerings with enthusiasm.*

He had been fortunate to receive scholarships to finish his schooling. Ironically, he would have been able to support his mother with his well-paying career as a medical researcher, but she had apparently found a benefactor who was able to provide more. While John always logically knew that his mother would need other men in her life, it was still a difficult pill to swallow.

He found relationships nearly impossible to sustain. There were women who showed interest in him, who took him up on the offer of dinner or a show, but it never progressed much further. Just as the other kids had sensed something unlovable about him, so did potential paramours.

Despite the loss of love from his mother, John continued his experiments regarding feline appetite in cases of leukemia or loss of kidney function. If he became famous for this research, she would hear about it. She would think of him and realize that she was wrong, that she missed him. Possibly that she loved him.

The initial trials led to a hypothesis that Solidox could help humans, especially those undergoing chemotherapy.

John had tried to distance himself from his subjects. He had tried to detach as a good scientist would. But the heart cannot stay guarded forever, and he found himself feeling fondness for Subject 12, who he lovingly called Miranda. Miranda had begun life as a plump Russian Blue, reminding him of Ollie, who he had liked so much in his mother's apartment. Miranda's disease had reduced her to a being no bigger than a beggar's wallet. At first, the Solidox primed her appetite. She was able to eat and digest small portions of wetted food and she heartily drank the cream that was offered to her.

When her eyes began to cloud over, Miranda lost interest in eating. The other cats were still responding well to the Solidox, with "well" scientifically corresponding to having an appetite within the "normal" range. It was a repeat of the Shadow experiment, with the disease outrunning the intervention. He did not want to tamper with the chemical compounds of the medicine, as there had been a high success rate, but he was confounded by the outliers. He began to suspect that his feelings of affection were clouding his judgement and introducing bias.

Solidox conclusively works as an appetite stimulant on mammals. Long-term repercussions are starting to appear.

John's job knew nothing of his research; they had no interest in animal pharmaceuticals. The consumers they wanted to garner were the ones with an urgency to impede the ravages of time. Market research had proven that women of a certain age spared no expense to conceal the fact that they had taken many trips around the sun. They were a demographic that would find indefinite resources to bury wrinkles, as if doing so warded off their own burials. John's company was pressuring him to create a clientele-based money-maker, and he had come up with absolutely nothing.

It was when he was agonizing over Miranda that he realized a solution was right in front of him. The cats, except for Miranda, had been faring well, but that did not mean the Solidox would work as well on humans. As a scientist, he knew he had to find a volunteer sample to test the product. Understanding his inherent lack of social skills, he wondered how he would go about accruing a decent sample. Also, there was something personal about the Solidox; it was the remaining connection to his mother. He felt vulnerable sharing it with the world until it was perfected. The last thing he wanted was for a failure to be made public.

He determined to try it first. He had no fear of anything bad happening. He trusted his intuition; he had faith in his hypothesis. His brain had always been loyal, and his knowledge was par none. With that in mind, he swallowed a pill.

He convulsed and he wondered if he should have taken it with water as a bitterness engulfed him. Then his stomach knotted.

He grabbed the side of the table he had been standing beside, holding himself up despite the sharp cramps. This lasted for several minutes until the knot unraveled and his stomach felt impossibly large, like an empty structure taking up most of the real estate in his body.

He tried to eat, but his throat seemed to have an open container of its own. His throat could not fill, nor could his stomach. Because of the food insecurity of his youth, he always shopped to excess and had more food in his pantry than he could possibly consume.

Or so he had thought.

John devoured boxes of noodles, cans of beans, and pieces of cooked chicken, but still his stomach growled, and his mouth drooled. He swallowed rice and soup; he deep-throated sandwiches and eggs. Still, he craved more. He ingested fish and chips, shrimp and grits, and biscuits and gravy. Nothing was able to touch the hunger.

He finally tore into one of the cans of cat food, as it was the only food left in his house. It partially sated him.

The limitation to the initial human study was that there was only one subject.

Even though Miranda's eyes were cloudy, John knew that she saw him. She saw him enter the room and she turned her face toward him. He sat beside her, comforting her. He petted her as she shivered. It was warm in his room where he had brought her; the shivers were from pain and not cold.

He had pentobarbital on reserve, but had been selfishly cuddling her for as long as she allowed.

His selfishness needed to end. He gave her a goodbye kiss between her ears. Miranda shuddered and sighed deeply. Her eyes rolled back before the needle broke her skin, as if she were racing the drug to the other side. He caressed her softly as her breath slowed and then stopped.

He had disposed of dozens of study animals, but he wanted something special for her. Something to mark her as special. As he was planning a memorial gesture, complete with flowers, his alarm went off. The alarm reminded him to take the Solidox, make note of his vitals, and record in his journal.

He gave Miranda another kiss before going to retrieve his pill. She was cooler to the touch already, and that broke his heart even more. He would do more than just flowers, he would build a monument, something permanent, something to remind him of the love he had felt.

He swallowed the pill. There were fewer cramps each time he ingested one. The hunger came quickly, and he bent over Miranda to cover her with a blanket before seeking sustenance. Her smell was decidedly different: decidedly delicious. Her scent was so appetizing, like stew that had been simmering all day. When he lowered his head to take a deep whiff, he swore it smelled like something a mother would make, like love, like goodnight kisses.

At least, that is what he thought he remembered goodnight kisses tasting like. It had been so long since he had received one.

He quickly moved away from her, before his appetite drove him to do the unthinkable.

Human subjects are seen to be converted to the diet of obligate carnivores. The study participants showed a change in gut enzymes as plant-based foods were no longer being required by their systems.

John had shelved the Solidox after being disgusted by his cravings. He stopped being a medical researcher and went into private practice, which offered him a comfortable level of popularity in his new island community. Eventually, a patient convinced him to revive the Solidox experiment. She explained how important it was for their bracket to remain viable, to maintain control over their environment and finances. She said that by helping others he was helping himself to a life of fecundity and fulfillment. She said much more, but what was most persuasive was that she reminded him of his mother.

With the patient, Nora, helping, John found that there was no shortage of willing volunteers for another study. It was documented that Solidox reduced the arthritic pain, the cataracts, the osteoporosis, and most of the negative side-effects of the aging process. The pill required high doses of protein, and it helpfully made any and all meat smell and taste delicious. Shortly after swallowing the tablet, the participants found themselves salivating over the nearest creature, finding live meat impossibly delectable.

This was the drawback of the pill, but one that Nora said was manageable. She waxed poetic about the circle of life and how, with Solidox, that circle could become larger for them. The participants agreed and the money that came in from the eventual sale of the pills certainly helped John to put his ethical dilemmas aside.

The final delimitation was that the experiments had begun with a bias: the researcher had wanted to gain his mother's adoration.

Chapter 4
The Gators Ate Ashes

"The gators ate ashes," Sidney said, clutching her teddy bear to her small chest as the neighborhood inhabitants sat gathered in the sunken concrete foundation, awaiting the storm. A reinforced roof had been erected for their safety, but they crouched as low as possible to heighten their chances of survival.

No one listening to the girl felt this statement was true, but it made sense. With each subsequent storm, the land was torn up to near scorched-earth levels. The thin and growing thinner livestock hunted unsuccessfully for plants and roots to gnaw on. The rabbits no longer scampered through yards, and people were forced to turn over their pets to shelters as they could not afford to feed them. The alligators, who normally benefitted from the domestic and non-domestic critters that roamed freely, would have little to eat.

"The gators ate ashes," the girl repeated. Whether this was some nontraditional nursery rhyme that she was mumble/singing to comfort herself remained to be seen. The discussion of eating was not welcomed, as most of the people taking refuge in the concrete shelter had not eaten for some time. They did not know where their next meal would come from, similar to the gators but unlike the human residents of Rodeo.

Rodeo residents stood out when shopping at the local grocery. Not only was their attire different, but their stockpiling methods were out of reach for those who had fished and farmed for generations. One woman, wearing a shirt that said *Boat Hair; Don't Care*, had loudly proclaimed to those closest to her in the store that she regularly bought food she did not plan to consume. It was part of her dieting protocol: to feel so comfortable with her surplus that she was not compelled to eat it. When someone suggested donating the extra to the food shelter, she had explained that she could never discard the food until it grew mold.

That was also part of the protocol.

Rodeo had been developed as a haven for those who had fled from the West Coast fires. The populace had taken the East Coast by storm and had seemed to bring storms with them. At first, the townspeople took kindly to the development, thinking it would help the local economy. They had read the sign and pronounced the name as one would pronounce an event where cowboys tried to remain seated upon a bucking bull. They had been corrected; it was to be pronounced in the same way as the shopping mecca in Beverly Hills. The people who lived in Rodeo cherished brands that the locals had never heard of. Rodeo residents wore things that sparkled and that were completely inappropriate for agricultural or marine work.

By the time this fourth and largest storm of the season was detected, the locals had been invited to wait it out in the area that had been cleared for the third Olympic-sized pool at Rodeo. The first two pools had become crowded, and local property taxes had been raised to accommodate the needs of the upper echelon. The locals had complained of the taxes but were now grateful for a solid base in which to hide from the deadly winds and detritus.

They sat in the concrete basin, the group of them. They had been gathered in what they assumed was the safest spot for them. They were banded together by fear, but honestly had little concern for each other due to recent events that had driven a wedge between families that had previously coexisted for decades.

"The gators ate ashes." Sidney was looking at Ellie even though her mother had asked her not to. Everyone avoided Ellie. They believed she was capable of black magic. They had heard she had made a pact with the Devil.

Before the seasons of the storms, when they had been faced with a nasty drought, children had disappeared, and they had blamed Ellie. They had claimed she held sacrificial ceremonies. They thought she made a pact for rain. She needed her crops to grow more than anyone. She was widowed and no one in town wanted to do business with her because of her relationship with the Devil. She needed to be able to ship her crops out; she needed the rain. They blamed her while the children continued to disappear until, finally, Ellie's own daughter had disappeared as well.

Sidney's mother put a hand on the girl's shoulder to quiet her. There weren't many children gathered in the empty pool, but those who were there were well behaved. Having friends and schoolmates disappear had a sedative effect.

"The gators ate ashes."

A few people *shushed* the girl as they felt the storm growing closer.

Someone had suggested that Ellie's daughter had been taken in retribution. After the girl had disappeared, it had rained. It had rained for so long that they began to curse it. Then the rain became storms, and they longed for days of just plain rain.

That the disappearance of the children started after the Rodeo residents arrived was ignored. The focus on Ellie was far more fascinating. She had carried the brunt of the rumor mill her entire life. She resembled the town pastor more than she did her father, and her husband's death had been mysterious.

Sidney rocked and clutched the teddy bear tighter. Her brother had been one of the first to disappear. Flyers had been posted in the grocery store, the post office, and the church. Flyers with different children's faces sprouted with the frequency of weeds. The townspeople prayed in church for the children's safe return. They inspected the fields before plowing, looking for oddly bent branches or footprints or any indication that someone had passed through. Or been dragged through.

The people of Rodeo were not interested in the flyers or the search parties. They lived on an entirely different frequency. They were a bottomless pit of need and their capacity for noticing the needs of others was limited to the point of being nonexistent. The Rodeo people were shiny and sparkly, and they drove cars that were both too large and too small. They had an impractical affinity for golf carts and thin cotton harem-style pants. They requested food be imported from places the grocer had never heard of. They wanted special tea and perfume and face cream. Their names had exotic pronunciations and they never attended the church services in town. When invited into conversations about the missing children, they seemed to believe it was only one child and that he was a runaway.

"The gators ate ashes." Ellie nodded at Sidney when the girl said this. Ellie understood; she closed her eyes and breathed deeply, and the storm picked up.

Then the rest of them understood. Sidney wasn't saying "ashes."

"The gators ate Ashley," she was saying, staring at the woman whose eyes remained closed. She was confessing, putting into words what she had witnessed, what had been done to the woman's daughter. The girl was confessing in the hopes of stopping the storm.

"What did you see?" Sidney's mother whispered. Even though she asked, she really did not want to know. She still hoped to find her son and rejected any information that would dwindle that hope.

The wind was directly above them. It howled with a ferocity that was chilling to hear. While the subtle rocking of the structure was disturbing, the sound was the worst part.

The children had disappeared on the grounds of Rodeo near where the townspeople were currently sheltering. Ellie had not been doing black magic; she had not made a pact with the Devil. She was only guilty of performing cleansing rituals, hoping to stop what was happening. While the rumors were correct in that she desperately needed financial security, her focus had been on trying to stop the children from being hurt.

Then her own child was hurt.

The night following a ritual with sage, moonflower, and white candles, Ellie had awoken to the sound of Ashley's scream. Running to her daughter's room, she found the window had been smashed and the girl's bed was empty. Ellie knew what was happening; she knew who was behind this. The Rodeo residents were becoming more brazen. They no longer waited for curious children to wander into the construction zone as if it were a house made of candy in the middle of an enchanted forest. They were violating the farms and rural homes and taking the children directly from their beds.

"The gators," Sidney whispered, and her mother remembered that that was the name her daughter had given to the old people of Rodeo. She thought their wrinkled skin, long noses, and sparse, sharp teeth made them resemble the reptiles that hid in the ponds near the farm.

A crack appeared in one of the walls of the pool, which caused the people sheltering within to gasp.

"It can't...collapse on us, right?" a woman named Callie, who had a missing daughter of her own, asked.

Several men looked overhead and placed their hands on the ceiling that had been positioned over the structure a few days prior. They felt around, trying to detect information regarding the stability of the roof. As they touched and deduced, a sound was heard from overhead. It was a wet, heavy sound, as if water could rap on a door and request entry.

"I don't think that is the storm," Bruce, a man who had positioned himself as far away from Ellie as possible, said. "I am not even sure we are feeling the storm at all."

"What do you mean?" his neighbor, both in life and in the pool, asked.

"It just feels...different. You know what the wind feels like, and this isn't it."

"Does someone want to take a peek outside?" Mark, a fisherman, asked.

"We shouldn't open the door during the storm," Callie said anxiously. "The winds could have some kind of...reverse effect and suction us out or something."

"Or blow off the door, leaving us more vulnerable," Sidney's mother offered.

Ellie was looking at the shut door and tilting her head, as if able to see through it. Sidney's mother wondered what the woman was sensing but knew better than to speak to her.

More time was spent touching the roof until someone suggested that the movement they were feeling had a deliberate rhythm.

"Wind doesn't act like that," Bruce confirmed.

"The storm passed already," Ellie informed them.

"It is directly above us. Heavy above us," Mark confirmed.

"The storm has passed," Ellie repeated.

"How do you know? You looking out a window?" Holden, who had started drinking when his twins went missing, subconsciously touched the flask in his shirt pocket.

Ellie shrugged. "It passed. The storm is over."

"Then why are we still feeling it?"

Ellie looked at Bruce, who lowered his head. Bruce had helped so many of them with restoration projects. His company had helped to lay the physical foundation for Rodeo. He had been both on the payroll of the out-of-towners and an integral part of the long-term community. He had solidified himself as part of the fold when his son disappeared. "I know that sound. It's concrete. Being poured.

"On us."

Chapter 5
Sparklers

Some might say the flies were the worst part. They congregated around the trash that had been neglected for weeks. The trucks belonging to the sanitation department had been overturned by the winds and the county was waiting for cranes to become available to right them.

Others might attribute their on-going psychological turmoil to the smells. There were a variety of distinct scents—none of them pleasant. Each smell climbed the olfactory ladder in a competition to reach the top. With the trash cans full, food had been left to spoil inside refrigerators which had grown warm during the month-long power outage. Wildlife victims of the hurricane had been left to rot in their dens and there were not enough carrion creatures to keep up with the demands of obliterating the corpses.

Some reported their biggest struggle being the lack of running water. Personal hygiene was on hold as water had to be scavenged for necessities like flushing the toilets. The irony of being on an island yet being in desperate need of water did not escape anyone. There was the famous "water, water, everywhere" quote that many thought of but refused to repeat.

For most, the worst part was the lack of communication. There was no television, no cable, no internet. Those on the island had no way of knowing if the news of their predicament was being reported.

Or if help was being sent.

They had no one to hear their complaints. No one to beg for assistance. Cell phone batteries had lost their charges long ago and only those of a certain generation had land lines.

"I have gas," Nicholas whispered, even though there was no one around to overhear. "We need to leave. We have to go."

Colleen nodded and pointed to the closed door of their daughter's bedroom. She had holed up in the room, in the dark, shortly after the winds had begun to blow, and had only ventured out to grab an occasional water bottle when they were fortunate enough to be able to secure them.

"She ran out of medicine over a week ago," Colleen said, lighting a tall candle that was originally intended for prayer. Now it was their major light source. "I hate how dark it is. It seems like we haven't seen the sun in ages."

"I like the dark. If not for the dark, we never would have had sparklers." He grinned mischievously.

She smiled. "The night we met. For the first time."

"The first of many."

She shrugged. "It took us a few turns to get it right."

They had first met at the age of twelve. It had been at a Fourth of July celebration. Colleen had been visiting her cousin, Susan, and had been dragged along to a community picnic. She had thought it was going to be boring: hearing about the other kids' shared experiences, listening to them talk about teachers she didn't know and places she didn't plan to visit. She had barely gotten out of the car in the parking lot when she had seen him. Nicholas had been running to catch a pass thrown by another boy. He was in a group of boys playing touch football, but she didn't register anyone but him. He had worn a soft t-shirt with navy blue piping and a rainbow decal on the front. His shorts had been crafted from khakis, and the legs that were exposed beneath the frayed edges told a story of summer exploits via scabs and bruises.

Susan had shoved her as she gawked at Nicholas running with the ball tucked beneath his arm. "We have to get in line for the funnel cake now, before the other kids finish their games and get in front of us."

While fried dough had been the one thing Colleen had looked forward to, she found that she no longer had an appetite. She wanted to stay where she was and marvel at this beautiful boy whose hair was thicker and wavier than any she had seen and who had lashes long enough to give you butterfly kisses from a few strides away.

Susan managed to link arms with Colleen and drag her to the refreshment truck. The parents sat on folding chairs and on benches, enjoying the freedom that a few dollars for snacks had bought them. The kids were expected to sit on blankets and eat and wait for the fireworks to begin.

Colleen craned her neck, seeking a glimpse of Nicholas, and was disappointed when she couldn't find him. She hoped his family hadn't left early.

"You gonna finish that?" A boy named Chad pointed to her funnel cake which she had barely nibbled on. She shrugged and passed it to him.

She leaned back and looked at the sky, watching the sun make its slow decent. As the sky darkened, a voice from behind her whispered, "I have a lighter."

She turned to find Nicholas holding a bouquet of sparklers in his hand. "We can light these, if you want."

She nodded and was relieved that it was dark enough to conceal the blush crawling up her cheeks.

Nicholas pointed to the row of fronds at the end of the field. "We can go over there."

Her heart skipped a beat.

"Where are you guys going?" Susan demanded.

"We're just going over there," Colleen said softly, silently begging her cousin to just let this moment pass.

Her pleas were ignored, and a loud announcement was made. "Oh, gross. They're probably going to go kiss or something."

The other kids within earshot sang a chorus of *"eeewwwww,"* but Colleen realized she didn't care. Let them think they were going to kiss. In fact, she hoped they would kiss.

There hadn't been a kiss that night, but there had been mini fireworks in the matter of the sparklers that they took turns holding. They wrote words in the sky; they drew dragons and cakes and a variety of small animals.

Nicholas had started to move away from her, and she was disappointed until he called, "Hey, Sparklers, come look."

She giggled. "That's not my name."

He shrugged and gestured to the ground where she saw a bird's nest that held three small eggs.

"Momma, Daddy, and baby," Nicholas said, pointing at each egg in turn.

She giggled. "That makes no sense. How could the parents be eggs too?"

"I guess it would just be nice for them to all be the same age together. Then they don't have to worry about anyone growing old first."

As illogical as that was, she had understood the sentiment behind it. She liked that Nicholas was a boy with feelings and that he was unafraid to express them. She liked Nicholas.

The time had come to leave the picnic and they had been too young to consider anything pertinent like exchanging phone numbers or addresses.

"Can you tell him to write to me?" Colleen had remembered the next morning when she was packing to go home.

"Nick? Eww." Susan scowled. "Why?"

Collen could no more explain why than she could capture the drawings made from sparklers on the sky. It seemed her request had been ignored, as no letters or postcards had arrived from Nicholas. Colleen settled back into life at home but still thought of the magical night with the sparklers, and the beautiful boy who had lit them, on occasion.

Years later, and after she had kissed several boys, Colleen decided to backpack across Ireland. Her parents were sternly against the trip, which made it even more appealing. She was legally an adult and paying her way with the money she had saved from waitressing, so they could do nothing more than voice their disapproval. When Susan heard about the trip, she mentioned that she had a friend who was doing a work exchange for the summer. She offered to put Colleen in touch with this friend to find out about the best places to sightsee and get cheap food and drinks. Colleen had been told to show up at a pub outside of Dublin and to look for a blond man wearing a jean jacket.

Being young and succumbing to the false sense of immortality that youth brought, Colleen had no worries about meeting up with a stranger in a place where she knew no one. Her biggest concern was that the pub would probably be full of blond men in jean jackets, and she would have to strategize how to find her personal information booth.

She did not have to strategize at all, as she recognized the man she should speak to right away.

He beamed and pointed at her. "Sparklers. Who would believe it?"

"I go by Colleen now," she joked, and was rewarded by his laugh. He looked the same, only taller.

"Sparklers is a perfectly fine name, though." He stood and pulled out the stool beside his so she could sit. "We should name our first child that."

She smiled the deepest and most sincere smile of her life. "I would like that."

They ended up naming their daughter Laoise, as they wanted something Irish to mark the place of their fateful reunion and the name means radiant girl or light, like a sparkler.

They had had sparklers on their wedding cake. No ceremony, just cake. The grandest they could afford. Sparklers were present for all birthdays and holidays, and the first thing they did at the beginning of every summer was to buy boxes of sparklers and burn them at night. They never grew tired of looking at the sky framed with flecks of burning gold.

"Tell Laoise to get in the car." Nicholas usually asked Colleen to relay messages to their daughter. Without her medication, Laoise was very difficult to talk to and she seemed to reserve most of her anger for her father.

Colleen knocked softly on the closed door. When she received no response, she cracked it open slowly, holding her breath as she always did out of fear of what she might find. Self-harm was not Laoise's signature, but she might be up for something new.

The room was dark, but Colleen could make out that it had been torn to shambles. There were clothes everywhere and drawers had been overturned. The girl, who was a woman now despite how Colleen saw her, was crouched down muttering about "yellow" and tossing items indiscriminately into opposite corners.

"Lee?" Colleen whispered. "We need to go. Dad said so."

Her daughter turned her head. Her eyes were rimmed red with exhaustion. "We can't go. I haven't gone through everything."

"Honey, it will be here when we get back. We just need to get over the bridge and see if we can find a place that still has power and water."

"We won't be back," Laoise said softly.

"Of course we will. This is a quick trip. We need to find out what is happening out there. Find out if supplies are being sent. It has been too long of a time without any information."

Laoise grabbed her hair angrily. "We won't be back. We won't. You might say we will, but we won't. Then what will happen to all this stuff?"

Colleen kneeled beside her and rubbed her back. "I promise. I promise we will be back. Wouldn't it be nice to find some hot food and take a shower?"

Her daughter lowered her hands and seemed to think for a minute. "You promise?"

"Cross my heart." With a little more cajoling, Colleen was able to convince her daughter to climb into the car's back seat.

Nicholas was peering out the front windshield as if looking for an indication of where to go. There were no signs or streetlights left, the hurricane had seen to that. "We'll drive north," he said decisively. "The hurricane veered off to the east, right?"

"I don't know. We lost power during the storm, and I haven't been able to find much out since then."

"We don't even know if there is anything left over the bridge," Laoise chimed in.

Colleen had to agree, but she decided to ignore the comment to maintain morale. "Do we have our papers?"

Nick pointed to the glove compartment. "They're in there, but no one will be in the tower. Nothing is up and running yet and the tower probably crumbled. Most of the houses did..."

They carefully navigated through roads that were partially blocked by fallen trees and street signs. They avoided the streets with downed wires or those that were still waterlogged. Eventually, they turned onto the road where the bridge would be visible if it were still there.

"It's completely gone." Nicholas said, astonished. "Why didn't anyone tell us?"

"How would they? No TV, no internet, we don't even have a battery-powered radio. The car couldn't pick up any stations, and we barely ran the car as there was no gas on the island." Colleen knew that everyone in the car was aware of these facts, but she needed to talk through them herself.

Nicholas pointed. "There are other cars up there, let's see what they know."

There were people standing outside parked cars, leaning on open doors and talking. In more fortunate circumstances this would appear as a social circle, as community members shooting the breeze. A closer look showed distress on the faces of those gathered. Gestures were made toward the gap where the bridge once was.

Nicholas pointed again. "That's Stan from the deli. He might know something."

"Yes, the deli is the communication hub of town." Laoise rolled her eyes.

"It kind of is, Lee," Colleen said, taking note of the familiar faces as they approached.

"Hey, Stan? Stan!" Nicholas called, and the man turned and waved them over. The group was standing with their backs to a pile of debris that was stacked nearly as tall as the tower had been before it had crumbled.

"When are they going to work on the bridge, does anybody know?"

A man next to Stan shook his head. "We haven't been able to get any news. Newspapers can't get over here. I only get one radio station and it's all music. Oldies. No DJ even, just plays songs on a loop."

Nicholas was beginning to formulate another question when Stan fell to the ground in front of them. A dart protruded from his neck.

"What the hell?" a woman said as people appeared from behind the debris, holding pipes and dart guns. They moved quickly, knocking into Colleen as they ran to drag Stan away from the group.

"What are those? What is happening?" Nicholas was turning his head in all directions, trying to make sense of the chaos.

"Look out!" Laoise pointed to the man with a dart gun that was aiming for her father. Nicholas was able to dodge the dart and Colleen grabbed his arm in one hand, Laoise's in the other.

They had left their car doors open and were able to dive back inside before any darts hit them. Nicholas slammed his foot on the accelerator and turned the car back toward home.

"Did you see that?" Colleen asked, keeping an eye on the pandemonium as they pulled away. She could make out struggling. There were several bodies on the ground with others bent over them. Those that were upright did not seem to be helping, but she could not persuade herself to believe what she thought she was seeing. "We can't even call for help. Should we swing by the police station?"

"I think we need to get home and lock the doors," Laoise said. "At least we still have a house to hide in."

It was not long before they learned that there would be no hiding. Days after the bridge incident, a woman came to their door, knocking with self-imposed authority. The woman refused to speak to Nicholas or Colleen, asking only for Laoise.

"Why should we let you talk to her? Who are you?" Nicholas stood between the woman and the open door, his arms folded. "We demand to know what is going on around here."

The woman stated robotically, "Communications will be reinstated soon. They are working on the infrastructure. In the meantime, we all need to abide by the rules, and it is evident that this household is not compliant."

"What does that mean?" Colleen asked. "We were just hit by a storm; we are trying to repair. We can't even reach our insurance—"

"It is not your physical house that is not compliant..." The woman peered past Nicholas' shoulder to see that Laoise was standing behind him. The woman pulled out a sheet of paper embossed with a strange seal. "Laoise Roman, it has come to our attention that you are still living at home. It is time for you to move out on your own," the woman read. "Adults do not live with their parents. Having to take care of oneself is good for motivation and for the financial and social economy of the island." She lowered the script, and sized Laoise up. "At your age, I had not lived with my parents for years. I was responsible for my own family, not simply sitting by and taking from others." Her words were tinged with disgust.

"You have no right to come here and—" Nicholas began.

The woman pointed to the seal on the paper. "I have every right." She focused on Laoise again. "You will feel better and more *useful* when you no longer have to rely on anyone. You may not even need to rely on...pharmaceuticals any longer when you are busy and fulfilled."

Laoise gasped. "How did you know—"

"You will be moved to an area for people your age. There are already people there. The ones without homes went first, and you will see that they are grateful for the shelter. You will see that they are living lives that are as fulfilling as possible, given the present situation. I believe you will find it to be liberating for you socially."

"We want her here." Colleen's voice caught in her throat.

"You are enabling her. Furthermore, it is now the law."

"What law?" Nicholas demanded.

"Statute 369, instituted three weeks ago."

"We have no way of knowing that; you could be lying. Who instituted it? Was there even a vote?"

The woman pulled her shoulders back so she appeared more formidable. "Rest assured that democracy carries on even during disasters."

Nicholas waved a hand at the woman, dismissing her. "If all that is true, if there is yet another surprise law around here, we will just pay the fine or whatever."

The woman narrowed her eyes. "I can assure you the punishment is far worse than a fine. I don't think you want to find out what it is."

Laoise spoke softly, "It's okay. I'll go."

"You don't have to." Her father continued to block her from the front door.

"She does," the woman interjected. She handed Laoise an envelope. "You are doing the right thing. You will find your address and keys in here. You have forty-eight hours to be completely moved."

Laoise had always been one to beat a deadline, it was one of her compulsions. She had managed to pull all her belongings together in thirty-six hours. She did not want any help from her parents with moving her boxes, only to borrow their car, which she returned promptly.

"The living quarters are close to town. I'll be able to get my necessities and keep my appointments easily," she explained, handing them the car keys.

"That's good," Nicholas said softly and without much conviction.

"Can they really do this?" Colleen asked. "How can they do this?" She felt as if she were trying to see stars on a cloudy night: nothing was transparent. It felt like nothing belonged to her anymore and that she belonged to nothing. They had struggled with the first rules; no one had liked the curfew or the cash-only requirement. They had fought against the paperwork to enter and leave the island. They had fought and lost. Never had she imagined families would be separated. Never had she imagined they would be held hostage in their own community.

Laoise agreed to taking her mother's bicycle, to make it a quicker trip back to her living quarters.

"We love you," Nicholas said as his daughter mounted the bike and began her wobbly trip down the road.

Laoise said nothing in return.

That night, Nicholas lit a sparkler to cheer up Colleen, but she was crying too hard to hold it.

"We will visit her. Every day, if you want," Nicholas said consolingly.

"It's not the same. We can't just leave, can we? I mean grab her and go somewhere else."

He shook his head. "There is no bridge and there are no more boats. I think most sank in the storm, but then the others..."

She nodded, understanding perfectly. "*They* took care of them. We have nowhere to go. No resources. We're sitting ducks."

The concept of sitting ducks was both prophetic and slightly off base. Colleen soon understood that they were more like livestock. After the living quarters edict was enacted, the colored bands were distributed. Every resident was required to wear an assigned band in much the same way that cattle are branded. The band had to be in view whenever the person wearing it was in public. At first the bands felt like a prohibitive collar, but, as with anything, the psychology of habituation was soon applied. People were grouped with those with like-bands and eventually it became natural to adopt a tribal mentality.

Then, the Solstices were ordered. Colleen realized that what they had witnessed at the bridge was simply the first unofficial Solstice. They, like everyone else, had been caught off guard when the rules were read, and they were ordered to leave their homes. Initially, people congregated, trying to come up with a joint strategy. They believed there was strength in numbers. What they didn't realize was that they simply made for a larger target. The Red Bands shot darts into the groups, knowing they would hit someone in the crowd.

The people then began to scatter, focusing only on saving themselves. This also worked in the Red Bands' favor. Isolated people were easier to corner, and when people stopped caring for the greater good, rules remained unquestioned.

Nicholas and Colleen stayed together during the premier Solstice, and the following day they regrouped with Laoise to try to determine a survival strategy.

"We do exactly what we did this time," Laoise insisted. "It worked. It will work again." She felt strongly against the three of them banding together while being hunted.

"But I want to be with you, they never said we have to stay within our coordinates," Colleen begged. "I can't focus knowing you are out there, in danger. I need to be able to see you."

"But we survived apart. That's why we survived. If we change anything—"

Colleen sighed, knowing her daughter's compulsions were inarguable. "What if you don't participate? What if you hide, maybe we find a weapon for you? Your father and I will participate, but you shouldn't."

Laoise shook her head. "They check the homes. You know that."

Colleen did know that. She was running out of options; no one on the island seemed to have any options.

Laoise lowered her eyes and placed her hand over her mother's. "We will be fine; I will be fine."

"I just..." Colleen choked back tears. "I love you."

The girl nodded but said nothing; her parents had grown accustomed to that.

The day of the fateful Solstice, Colleen had a premonition of dread. She sat beside her husband, waiting for the announcement. She was shaking when she said, "Remember when we found that nest when we were kids and you mentioned it was good for everyone to be the same age so we don't have to worry about anyone growing old first?" When he nodded, she continued, "Now growing old sounds like bliss. And if Lee could just watch us do that—"

He took her face in his hands. "She will."

When the announcement ended, they stood and walked to the door holding hands.

"We will go to the Lavender quarters," Nicholas stated.

"She doesn't want us there."

"Doesn't matter. We have to do what is best for her. We have to protect her. It's probably better for us, anyway. If we have learned anything, it's that they go for Green Bands when possible."

"It's a long walk."

He smiled and she was reminded of the smile he had given her at that picnic an entire lifetime ago. "I've got all night."

Nicholas had been right about many things in their years together and he was right about the Green Bands being targets. They had not made it far when they realized they were circled by four Red Bands. It was like a blasphemous double-date. The men were dressed in their golf outfits, the women in sequins and sandals. They pointed their dart guns but were still a few yards away and waiting to get closer before pulling the trigger.

Colleen felt Nicholas take a deep breath. He met her eyes and said, "Hey, Sparklers, I have a lighter." Before she could respond, he pushed her into the bushes. Then he pulled a sparkler from his pocket and lit it.

He began to wave the glowing stick and call to the Red Bands, taunting them. As she watched him run, Colleen swore he was drawing dragons in the sky. And a cake. And her name with a heart beside it. He was every bit as beautiful as when she had first seen him.

Eventually he stumbled. Even from a distance, she could see darts stuck into him. He rolled onto his back, and that was the last movement he made. Two of the Red Bands fell on top of him. She could hear the Red Bands making sounds that she did not want to assign meaning to.

She was lost. Even though she was on a street she had traveled more times than she could count, she was adrift. She could not remember making decisions without her husband's input. She could not remember a time when she had put her needs ahead of Nicholas or Laoise.

She was also lost in the sense that she had lost. She knew there was nothing she could do. She also knew she could not live without Nicholas. He had been the only boy she had loved.

There was no room for love during Solstices, so there was no room for Colleen. As awful of a wish that it was, she wished that Laoise would realize that anxiety and compulsions would also not survive during this terrible time. She didn't know if Laoise would ever learn of what happened this night, but she hoped she would understand the choice Colleen was going to make and realize that choices were available.

The two Red Bands that were not busy with her husband were heading toward her. Colleen refused to give them what they wanted. Nicholas had sacrificed himself to protect her; she would not let him down.

They would not have her; she would not be their meat.

She turned and walked into the nearest residence, knowing they would follow and being fully aware of the rules.

Chapter 6
Log Rolling

When The Fifth collapsed, Nora's husband collapsed along with it. The Fifth had been a luxury complex with architecture not seen before. The structure had been named after the street in New York, a place that conjured exotic images to the Midwesterners who would benefit from the building. The Fifth had incorporated shops, cafes, and financial offices in a swirling mandala pattern that stood higher than any other structure in the vicinity. It had been grand enough to spot from airplanes. At night, the lights radiated for miles, dampening the very stars in heaven. Nora's husband had been a curator of dreams, a creator of opulence, an artist who worked in the medium of lavishness.

He was considered a casualty of the faulty foundation, even though he had been nowhere near it when it had crumbled and had lived for three weeks after its plummet.

Nora never loved him more than she had in those three weeks, when he was completely devastated, completely vulnerable. He had perfect use of his limbs, was mobile without hinderance, yet she fed him and bathed him and brought him a bedpan. And when he eventually said that he wanted his gun, she made sure it was loaded. She had oiled it so it wouldn't catch. She had kissed him on the forehead before he put the muzzle in his mouth. She didn't have to help him with this part. Nor did she bother to stick around to clean their home of his blood and brains. There was always someone else willing to clean up or forced to clean up. She never knew the difference, nor did she care. She headed east, as most everyone had been doing.

"It's a small world and getting smaller," Nora had told herself as she strategically placed her sun visor around her perfectly coiffed hair. She had been a hairdresser in a different lifetime. When she had met her first husband, she had put her combs and scissors in storage. She was able to pay for someone else to do her hair. She was able to pay for someone else to do her cooking and cleaning. She was able to pay for extras and for perks that others only wished for. She was able to do this because of her skill of marrying well.

Once east, she married a politician. He was a planner, a doer, a man with a legacy. His eldest son had succumbed to cancer, and this had crafted a narrative of emotional resilience and personal faith that voters found attractive. The politician had a younger son who despised Nora at first glance, which had only fueled her desire to win the love of the politician. Once she became Mrs. Politician, she involved herself in her husband's work. She made site visits, she participated in campaign events, she shook hands with important people and offered suggestions of how to secure her husband's endorsement.

She was not happy with the younger politicians that she was forced to play nicely with. They seemed brutish and uncouth. They focused on the environment and mental health issues instead of making sure Social Security would still be available or fighting inheritance tax. She would complain to the politician, but he suggested that maybe he and Nora were "dinosaurs" and not seeing things from the mindset of someone with most of their life in front of them.

She tried to understand the younger mindset. She examined social media posts, online videos, and blogs. What she found was mind-numbingly vapid. She wanted someone to commiserate with, but months of perusing the pathetic misuse of social media by her peers showed that her age group was not much better. They wasted time complaining of poor service in restaurants and of the driving habits of others. They had lost interest in doing anything substantial. The same people who had made great strides in the 1960s and 1970s no longer wanted to change the world.

Nora was a champion of change. She saw how a certain age group was being put out to pasture and no longer taken into consideration. She was not going to sit idly by and watch the desired platforms of her demographic be shelved. They were people, not products with an expiration date. She had honed her skill of manipulation on her husbands; she could apply it on a larger scale. Most of her social circle were nice people who were satisfied with what they had and the lives they had lived. The one common denominator was that no one was a fan of growing older. They put on a brave face and talked about this "season of life," but no one enjoyed the aches and pains and the overall feeling of loss that accompanied it. Nora, especially, hated growing old, and was motivated in prolonging it at any cost.

She invested in MLMs that involved creams and tinctures. She quickly assembled a downline of bored people who worried about maintaining wealth in a life that was long, but who held longevity in the highest regard. She used social media to energize her troops and keep them selling and providing her with passive income. She became flush in her own money, which she fed into a private account. She no longer had to sugar up her husband for any extras. This was what it meant to be an independent woman. This was how it felt to be fully in charge.

She grew to despise the competition, the other products with flush downlines and customers clamoring for product. She saw them cannibalizing her profits and knew that they must be stopped. She spoke at her company meetings and cruises; she ramped up her social media posts. She incentivized in ways that had not yet been discovered. She acted as general, leading her troops to take out the enemy by outworking them.

Then she went for the source.

Factory fires were not unusual. Leggings burn quickly and essential oils combust easily. The optics of a woman at a certain age, unphased by her boat hair, directed suspicions away.

Money flowed easily for Nora and her followers. She was called an inspiration. She was a widow who had gone on to love again, to find life again. In the shops, in the hair salon, on the pickleball courts, she sermonized. She played on the fatigue and fear of those around her. She promised security. She explained that there were ways for them to remain important. She claimed that they did not have to hand over their power simply because they were of a certain age.

She motivated the retired to get involved again. She eased them into her ideas, promising comfort. There was nothing sinful about wanting comfort.

She told them what posts to look for, buried in the banality of senior social media groups.

JUST WANTED TO KNOW IF ANYONE IN THE NEIGHBORHOOD CROCHETS.

This post was embedded on the background of a person holding a birthday cake and wearing a birthday hat.

Nora didn't mind that the youngsters she had "friended" made fun of the mismatch between the message and the background. Those that she wanted to reach understood the message she was trying to communicate.

@Boathair my grandmother tatted...she made the most beautiful handkerchiefs and tablecloths...I can't help you with crochet, but I can give you some of her old patterns if you want to tat. LOL.

The word *crochet* translated as a plan to monopolize business. Followers were being instructed on which businesses they could patronize and which they were to freeze out. Tat was in reference to secret meetings on the island about which politicians to favor. The politicians were part of the meetings and were told of the issues they were to promote. The judges were told how to vote, and the stores were told what items to import. Nora was largely in charge of these decisions.

Daryl's has the best all-day breakfasts. This message had a unicorn backdrop.

Following a minor storm, posts about Daryl's began surfacing in both private groups and on main pages. The storm had left the area without power for a considerable amount of time, during which life had to return to one of using cash or checks to make purchases. Once power was restored, the Daryl's posts lobbied for maintaining a cash-only existence.

"It's so much simpler now," Nora assured those who complained about the loss of debit card machines. "Besides, no one trusts banks anymore. We should all be considerate and protective of our digital identities. Cash cannot be 'hacked,' it is the purest form of currency."

Once the cash-only protocol was established, businesses were persuaded to incorporate in-person-only transactions. The internet was to be used solely for messages and social communication. The island would be known for its quaintness. Tourists would flock for the chance to go back in time, for the opportunity to disengage.

The prediction came true; tourists visited and spent money freely. Most fell in love with the island and lamented returning home. Then, the fires started in the western part of the country and some no longer had homes to return to. The need for Rodeo was born in this manner.

"Life is certainly more civilized now," Nora told the politician. "But we need to work to maintain order. The fires are pushing everyone to this coast. Soon our little island will be overrun."

"We have plenty of space," he assured her. "The golf courses can be converted into additional housing. Something like The Fifth, remember that?"

Nora snorted. "It's not the space, darling, it's the *resources*. And it is the duty of...people like us to be guardians of the resources. One look at our assets demonstrates an elevated skill for...fair distribution and living comfortably."

The politician smiled kindly. "I am not sure I agree with you, my love. Frugal living, minimalist living might be what is best for the greater good. That would assure that we have necessities available for all."

Nora scowled. "We have worked hard. Why should we give up all we worked for?"

He patted her hand. "I love how protective you are of us, like the prettiest guard dog there is. The truth is, you and I won't be around long enough to see the worst of it."

This comment spiked Nora's ire. How dare he suggest she had little time left? While that may be true for him—being a man and being a few years older than she—she faithfully committed to her products. She drank the chalky vitamin drinks, she swallowed the herbal supplements, she applied the invigorating overnight poultices. If anything, she was aging in reverse.

Had an omelet for the early bird special... This was seen written over a woman holding a bullhorn.

Omelet was a term used to seek support for a law outlawing adolescents from working. There were adults on a fixed income who needed the part-time shifts to cover their bills at Rodeo. The bullhorn represented college students and the bill to prevent them from holding employment while in school. Dedication to studies meant exactly that. Students would have plenty of opportunities to pay their education loans after graduation. Nora had never attended college, but her husbands hadn't carried any debt from their advanced degrees. She knew that financial feasibility simply required gumption.

Love Daryl's! Yum. This was placed on a background that was a sea of footballs.

Yum was a reference to the papers required to enter the island. The footballs represented the papers needed to leave.

"It's not a matter of keeping track of everyone," Nora answered when posed with questions at the meeting at the Antler's Club. "It's assuring we maintain stabilization. It...protects our beaches and the environment."

"We need people coming to this island to maintain business," someone called out.

"Have you watched the news?" Nora scoffed. "Tourists no longer exist. There are people who have things, like us, and people who want what we have. How many of you have security cameras on your homes?"

All hands were raised.

"Checking papers at the bridge is the same as a security camera. And having someone to check papers creates even more jobs for us."

"Why do we need to check people leaving?"

Nora had prepared for this. "Carbon footprint. We can't have people joy-riding on and off the island. People are permitted to leave for work, or they can apply for a permit due to extenuating circumstances. Before you know it, this will all seem normal." She smiled, knowing this was true. Everything else she had suggested had been incorporated and had become habitual.

She continued, "We mostly use electric golf carts. We are doing our part in preserving this beautiful island for our descendants. Our carts are quieter, cleaner, and they smell better. Having them has allowed us to shut down that eyesore of a gas station—"

"Deluca's?"

"Yes. They also charged an arm and a leg for bagels and coffee. We are all better off at Daryl's."

It wasn't difficult for Nora to convince her people to listen to her, nor was it difficult for her to get her husband to campaign for the issues she was purporting. The politician catered to her. He adored her. A few butterfly kisses with her heavily mascara-ed eyelashes coerced him to agree to anything. In this sense, Nora considered herself a type of sequin-clad founding father. She had played an integral part in metaphorically paperclipping the rider for new laws to a bill for salary increases for teachers, social workers, and professional caregivers. All of the active voters had all been influenced via social media and the bill passed unanimously.

The politician began to forget the codes and the new rules. He spoke to Nora as if she were his first wife and they were just beginning their marriage. He had difficulty remembering his appointments or who he was meeting for golf.

She had never loved him more than when his mind started to fail. He was even more pliable when he had the organizational skills of a toddler. Then he became a burden. He was no longer able to do things for himself, and she did not like when people could not do things for her. She told his son that she could no longer care for the politician. The man who had spent decades shaking hands and kissing babies would be ending his days in a nursing home, completely forgetting he had signed divorce papers.

Nora, armed with the excitement of living in a brave, new world, put herself out there. She remained active in the Antler's Club, the Caribou Lodge, and the Silver River Gambling Association. She made sure she was seen in places where single men of a certain age and economic bracket congregated. It wasn't long before she met and became betrothed to a judge. He was a man of vision who had an astounding track record of overturning laws that had become so incorporated as to be second nature for the culture.

At one of their canasta matches, Nora began talking to those playing about the pills she had learned about. She explained that their shared physician was also a renowned scientist and that he had whipped up a major miracle in his lab. She told them that he was in possession of a longevity pill. She explained that it reversed aging, that it increased sexual stamina, that it would make them the *final* generation.

Ken has succumbed to the cancer. LOL.

In senior jargon, LOL meant lots of love. For the people in the know, it meant that Solidox was now available. Nora began coordinating medicine distribution, using fake events like Bingo and Keno to tell her followers where and when to secure the elixir.

They took the pills as instructed: one every few months. Nora often took hers with a shot of brandy. The first time she had taken one, it took some time to register the effects. Each subsequent trial found the insatiable hunger settling in sooner and stronger. The hunger became overwhelming, and she and the judge would reduce their pantry to crumbs. One night on Solidox, she and the judge had raided the buffet at Silver River along with the late-night Chinese take-out, but the hunger remained.

The judge had rubbed his stomach and whined. She was not attracted to him when he showed weakness. "I'm still hungry," he complained.

"We all are," she retorted, "not just you." She hated when he made it all about him, instead of making it all about her.

"Let's get in the golf cart and drive around. There must be something open. McDonald's or something."

Nora sighed and straightened her hair even though there was not a strand out of place. "Let me pick the radio station though. I am not listening to sports." As she walked toward the cart, she nearly tripped over a cat that was lying in the middle of the alley.

"What is wrong with that?" The judge pointed at the mass of sticky fur.

"I think it's hurt."

"Is it dead?"

"No. It's breathing." She kneeled compulsively. Normally, she would not sacrifice her slacks to the dirty alley, but there was something about the cat that was compelling. She wanted to touch it, pull it close to her. She bent over and sniffed.

"You're smelling it?"

She nodded. "It smells good."

He wrinkled his nose. "That's disgusting."

She beckoned him with one taloned finger. "Come here."

"I will not."

She lowered her voice to the seductive tone she used to coax him into taking Viagra. "It smells like...like the roast my mom used to make, like chocolate cake, like a dirty martini."

He slowly crept toward the feline. "How can it smell like all of that?"

She leaned over and sniffed again. "I don't know, but it does. It smells...delicious."

As if the cat knew what Nora was saying, it gave a weak growl and tried to crawl away. The judge and Nora worked together and were able to staunch their hunger in a manner that neither of them would have been proud of if not compelled by the Solidox.

The day following the cat's consumption, Nora's skin looked younger. Her eyes appeared fresher. On subsequent visits to casino night, she obtained more pills and found more cats and decided that the entire experience was one she deserved.

I do not give this page permission to show anything of mine. That includes pictures.

This message was posted several times a day by unique users, who always followed the post with an unrelated picture or a message about new furniture they purchased. These messages allowed for planned hunting. Until the hunting became exhausting and dangerous. Until the cats no longer satisfied. Nora found she could consume several cats in one night and still feel the hunger. She craved bigger game. She became despondent.

With her seductive voice, she asked the judge to take his Viagra. Sex always cheered her up. They had long since abandoned undressing each other and simply discarded their clothing quickly, allowing the candlelight to let them pretend that stretch marks and wrinkles did not exist. She climbed on top of him, as she usually did, and began rubbing his chest and abdomen. She felt him grow hard beneath her, but her interest remained on his abdomen. She believed she could feel the smooth contours of his intestines twisting and turning against her fingers as she traced them over his loose skin. She imagined herself slurping the long line of the small intestines just as she would a long piece of linguini. She remembered how the cats had tasted and how they had smelled. She leaned closer to his navel and inhaled. He smelled sweaty in a way that was unusually pleasant. She licked at his stomach, letting his body's sodium soak into her tongue.

He put his hand on the top of her head and tried to compel her to move her mouth lower. Instead, she took a roll of flesh between her teeth and carefully bit down.

"What are you doing?" He sat up, knocking her off him.

Confusion reigned, so entranced she had been in his smell and taste. Then she began to piece together what had happened. As she rode him, her mind drifted, puzzling through recent events. Licking him had made her feel better. She fantasized about the effect of swallowing parts of him.

Nora had never loved the judge more than when she was adding hemlock to his tea. The paralysis allowed her to taste him at her leisure. His intestines had been everything she had imagined. The fingers that had once caressed her slid down her throat easily. His eyes had somehow been juicier than the cats' and his tongue had tasted exquisitely different outside of his mouth than it had when she had kissed him.

She had never loved the judge more than when he was inside of her, than when she was digesting him and noting the effect the protein he donated had on her physically and mentally.

As the judge became elimination, her love for him was also eliminated and she became lonely.

Does anyone know what kind of snake this is? I spotted it on my bougainvillea.

Snake was a code representing those outside of the Solidox circle. Bougainvillea related to a discussion regarding instituting an island-wide curfew.

One night at backgammon, while Nora was receiving her pills from Dr. John, she mentioned how she had used hemlock to make sure she could devour her prey without hurting herself. He listened attentively and it became clear that he realized she was not talking about cats. It also became clear that he was an attractive man for his age. He asked her to come to his home so they could discuss things further. With each visit, he explained the research he had been doing on ways to safeguard paralysis. He was using pentobarbital and was toggling with the doses. With each visit he explained more about what the victims would be able to feel while being consumed. With each visit, their relationship developed, as the heart cannot stay guarded forever. When Nora told him she loved him, he received the information enthusiastically.

They became inseparable and began gathering their meals together during Solstice. They had a routine: charcuterie and champagne, love songs on the radio, and then the main course. Their record for obtaining sustenance had been impeccable until John had introduced a twist: go after a woman he had drugged with something special. The failed research on his part had led Nora to question if the doctor were not experiencing the same decline the politician had.

"What made you try that?" she had asked him after they had dropped the lavender-banded woman off in front of her living quarters. They were not concerned about anyone scavenging her, the drugs she had been administered had caused her to smell awful.

He shrugged. "I was bored. I wanted to experiment. It's what scientists do; they experiment."

She pursed her lips. "Not on Solstice. This is not the time to take risks."

"Risks?" He laughed and pointed to the red band around his neck. "We are untouchable, my dear. I guess I just wanted to try something, and I hoped for the best. It's what I always do."

"This time, your best was way off."

"I wanted it to taste like goodnight kisses."

"You keep saying that. It's ridiculous. How can something taste like a kiss?"

"More like the way the kiss makes you feel."

"You can't taste a feeling."

They rode in their golf cart in silence. The cart drifted over traffic lines and Nora wondered if this was the beginning of some neurological issue with John or if he was simply hungry.

"I see something." She pointed to a woman who was near the grocery store by the Blue Band living quarters.

They pulled over and the woman began to run. Nora was not one to miss and her dart found the Blue Band's neck, knocking her to the ground. Soon, Nora and John were on her. They were outside the grocery store, which would be problematic for crime due to the security cameras, but Solstice had its own rules. They had been so hungry and agitated over their failed attempt to find nourishment that they began to pummel the woman, which had the desired effect of tenderizing her meat. Nora started as she usually did by drinking the blood, keeping her food alive and alert as it was tastier with adrenaline. Then she moved to the abdomen, biting through the tender flesh and fat covering the stomach and pulling out the entrails. John started at the feet, first sucking the toes, and then crunching on them one by one.

She looked at him and smiled. "This little piggy..." she sang in a childish voice.

He stopped chewing and thought for a moment. "I don't remember how that goes."

She straddled the woman and looked him in the eye. "You don't remember it, or you never knew it? Think, John." The woman beneath her was still breathing, which was miraculous, but Nora's mind was focused on more important matters.

"I knew it once," John replied, moving up to the woman's head and sucking out an eyeball. He had a fondness for eyes.

"You were the first to take the Solidox... Do you think this..." she tapped the side of her head and then pointed to his "...is a side-effect?"

Dr. John looked confused, and his eyes were moving rapidly. Nora would not allow for his failing state to shift the concern away from her. "What I'm asking is, will what is happening to you happen to me?"

"What do you mean? What do you think is happening to me, Nora?"

"You are losing your mind, just like my husband the politician. The Solidox didn't help him, but he was already senile when he began to take it. That makes me wonder about you... I didn't notice it, but were you senile before, John?"

"I took the Solidox years ago in the first trial. I told you that. There is nothing wrong with the pills."

She bit into the woman's bicep and chewed thoughtfully. "John," she said, once her mouth was clear of muscle, "remind me, how did we meet?"

"Us? How we met?" He was obviously stalling. "We were introduced at the Auxiliary."

"And the Solstices, do you know when the next one is?"

"Is this a quiz?" He opened the woman's mouth and took a bite out of her tongue. "I have no idea when the next one is, do you?"

Naturally, she knew exactly when the next Solstice was scheduled as she was the one who scheduled them. Dates were not released far in advance, to keep everyone on their toes, but there was a set schedule.

He sat back and rubbed his stomach. "I'm getting full. That is a first."

It was indeed a new response. Nora continued eating, feeling the pangs of hunger rumble on. She had gathered the information she needed, and she had never loved him more than in that moment. She had always been two steps ahead of him, but now she was advancing, evolving, and rapidly leaving him behind. For all of John's book smarts, she had always been more cunning, more creative. She had always been out of his league.

She reduced the woman to bones and bits, and they climbed back into the golf cart to return home. During the silent drive, Nora remembered the exchange she had shared by the pool in Rodeo with the dashing movie director who had been stranded on the island during the storm. She made a mental note to pay him a visit during one of John's frequent naps.

Chapter 7
Rejoice Because Thorns Have Roses

After the Late Spring Solstice

Nancy felt blessed to have Ava as a neighbor. The woman was personable and bright, and she often picked things up at the Day Market for Nancy on her way home from work. Ava provided beautiful flowers for the yard behind their living quarters. It was important to maintain value in a world where Red Bands doled out favors, but also dangerous when they simply took what they desired.

The two women were drinking sweet tea amongst Ava's roses and enjoying the blue skies and warming sun. It had been a few weeks since the Solstice, which meant they could relax until the next one was ordered. Solstices were held at the whim of the Red Bands, as opposed to following the position of the sun. They were announced if there was an economic need or health requirement, and the time in between typically contained an undertone of celebration.

"Believe it or not, this is one of the busiest times at the store," Ava was saying. "I had to do an arch for the entrance of the golf tournament, a life-size flowered bingo board for the Antler's Club, and table garnishes for the Ladies' Auxiliary."

Nancy leaned forward. "When you have to work with...*them*, are they creepy?"

Ava shrugged. "My energy is focused on appearing indispensable."

Nancy nodded. She knew that Ava was appreciated by the Red Bands. She also knew that Ava made more money than most of the Green Bands. While Ava remained a resident of the Green Band living quarters, rumor was that she paid for protection on Solstices, meaning she paid to be invisible.

Literally.

Nancy wanted to ask if the drugs Ava took had side-effects. She honestly didn't care, but wanted to open the door for talk of maybe trying a pill. Possibly during the next Solstice. Ava had no reason to protect Nancy or to be generous with her resources, but they were friends.

Before she could ask, Ava returned the conversation to her flowers. "I know people think that horticulture is challenging work, and it is, but really the flowers ask so little of me."

Nancy nodded. Before the Solstices began, she was married. Much of her time had been focused on her relationship and on her wife. They had been a great team, but communication and compromise had been required. Reward came from emotional labor in that Nancy's marriage had been one of mutual trust and admiration. Ava's relationship with her flowers was, by nature, one-sided, and Nancy found it sad that Ava seemed to receive her sole fulfillment from that.

"Those are my newest...experiment. I've been playing with the color."

Nancy laughed. "Lavender, like the bands? You trying to subliminally make lavender appealing?"

Ava put a finger to her lips as if they were sharing a secret.

Nancy peered at the bush that was on Ava's left. "It really is extraordinary, how you get the colors to be so rich, so deep."

"I have a secret ingredient."

"Yes, you always say that." Nancy looked at the bush behind Ava's head and sighed, thinking again of relationships and how much loneliness she faced as a widow. The Solstices had robbed everyone in some way. "Blue roses are sort of sad, aren't they?"

Ava seemed to consider this. "They are better than yellow ones. Yellow always brings complications."

"I never thought of that..." Nancy made a lot of allowances for Ava's strangeness. From the stories Ava told, it seemed that she had few social outlets even before the new normal. It had always been her and the flowers.

"Think of the stoplights," Ava explained. "Red and green have clear orders. You know exactly what to do when you see those colors. Yellow is confusing. Do you speed up to see if you can beat it? Do you slow down only to have other people angry because you paused when you should have accelerated? It's an entirely complicated color." Ava sighed. "And yet I grow the yellow ones. Others demand them, and I am all about supply and demand."

"I like this one the best." Nancy pointed to a coral-colored bush behind her chair. "This color is amazing, like a sunset. You've really outdone yourself." She reached toward the rose, only to snag her finger on a thorn. "Can I...?" She pointed to the back door which led to Ava's rooms. Her own back door was locked, as they had walked through Ava's home to their seats among the roses, and Nancy would have to walk to the other side of the compound to reach the front entrance to her apartment.

"Of course. I have some bandages in the bathroom."

As Nancy was tending to her finger, she once again marveled at how lucky she was to score Ava as a neighbor. They enjoyed each other's company and Ava was always so helpful. Nancy dried her hands on the guest towel and placed a bandage on her cleaned finger. As she threw the bandage wrapper away, she noticed there were bloodied towels stuffed in the bathroom hamper.

"My roses appreciate your donation."

Nancy hadn't noticed Ava enter the bathroom behind her. "I usually have to work so much harder for my fertilizer," the woman said, reaching around Nancy's chest, and pinning her arms to her sides. "I am so lucky to have such a helpful neighbor," Ava whispered in her ear. The sharpened pruner was the last thing Nancy saw.

Three Solstices Prior

Ava liked to tell jokes at the flower shop, calling herself a *budding* comedian. The jokes were welcomed by the Red Bands, who enjoyed a good rib-tickling on all days, but especially when they gathered bouquets for victims' families. Not everyone sent flowers, but the ones who retained some sense of humanity felt an obligation. At first, they tried including cards with the roses, but there truly were no words appropriate for the situation. Ava's jokes would have been completely tone deaf, so the flowers spoke for themselves.

Ava was not social by nature, so the jokes were an easy way to fill any awkward silences. For instance, she might call a customer "bud," or talk about a sudden "change of plants," or where her "issues stem from." She would wink and say she was just "pollen their leg."

The one thing Ava would never joke about were the roses. They were the best of their kind, due to their fertilizer. Before the hurricane, she had shown her flowers in other cities, in other states, in places that no longer existed or were no longer accessible. She resented that her fame was now limited to her Rodeo customers, but she was grateful that they found her necessary.

The secret ingredient had been discovered before the time of the Solstices. It had been harder to acquire then—or, at least, harder to get away with. The secret ingredient had been found due to the tiny weapons roses carry on their stems that can cause blood loss for those not paying attention. Especially for those working in literal pounds of roses daily. It was not long before Ava pieced together a connection between the roses she had bled on and the ones the customers raved about. Her few little drops of blood had provided a certain sheen, a certain luminescence that made the flowers desirable.

The flower shop was conveniently located near the hospital, which kept business "blooming" and blood flowing. In the days before the Solstice, flowers were practically mandated for hospital visits, hence the flush business. The blood had come from Ava's phlebotomist friend; it was the rush that made the roses blush.

Then, Ava had no longer been permitted to receive bags of blood. Her friend said something about suspicions. Something about the factory accident and triage. Something about their friendship being one-way and his no longer wanting to risk his job in return for her lackluster affections.

She only felt true affection for her flowers.

She had basically ignored all her friend said but had focused on the word *triage.*

Arriving at accidents ahead of emergency personnel had been easy. She had a scanner in the office at the shop, and she knew which of the police, firemen, and EMTs in the area were slow on the draw. Since these were accidents, the blood was not needed for evidence: no one missed a few ounces.

Or even a little more.

That met Ava's, and the flowers', demands until the new normal. The new rules put everyone in danger. Ava needed to garner positive attention and meet the requirements of people whose satisfaction was hard to secure. Ounces of blood would no longer suffice.

Accidents would no longer suffice.

Just as *triage* had caused an epiphany, the horror of the Solstice had inspired a change in business plan. The Red Bands left little of their *food* behind for scavengers, but those that were executed were dumped unceremoniously. Those that hid from the ceremonies became her supply chain.

She simply had to survive the Solstice in order to protect her roses.

She had been lucky so far. Many Red Bands recognized her and would allow her to pass and seek other sustenance. They needed their flowers, and they knew there was not a large talent pool to pull from if she were eliminated. For this Solstice, she had crept about, mostly keeping hidden, waiting for the gunshots that announced an execution. Like most, she kept moving. Any other approach was suspicious. Her movement naturally led to her shop. This was the path she took almost daily. Being outside the shop was an additional form of torture; she was not allowed to enter and look at her flowers.

The area was mostly deserted as the night was wearing on and many of the Red Bands would have already acquired their meals. She was not completely alone on the street, as she noted one man looking directly at her. She recognized him from the shop and felt comfortable that he would recognize her.

It had been a while since he had been in her shop and he looked smaller, more shrunken, than he had before. This was surprising, as Solidox was supposed to counter the effects of aging. The man had an uncertain gait. As he passed beneath a streetlight, Ava could see that his face held an expression that was equally uncertain.

The man staggered to her and tapped her on the shoulder. "This bridge traffic is maddening, bumper to bumper."

Ava didn't move. The man's confusion was unnerving. Perhaps he didn't recognize her. She was waiting for him to reach for his dart gun. Instead, he kept talking. "I was expecting you, Nora. I thought you would never get here."

Ava nodded, still not moving.

"I have a full tank of gas, Nora. We could be off this island and someplace better in the blink of an eye." He looked wistfully into the dark night around him. "It's hard to get gas, you know? One time, I sat in line from seven-thirty in the morning until three in the afternoon waiting for a turn at the pump. It was a full day of work, just waiting for gas."

Ava realized this man did not mean to harm her. He was also completely removed from reality. She remembered they used to call it "sundowning" when older people would lose all recall toward the end of the day.

The night had been wearing on and there hadn't been any executions that she knew of. Her roses could not be bargained with; their needs could not be put on hold simply because their supply of fertilizer was not available.

Ava looked around: there was no one in their area, close to the shop. She felt as if she were facing a yellow traffic light. Should she stop and wait or accelerate? She laced her arm through the man's. "I think leaving is a good idea. Let me grab my bag."

"Oh good." The man smiled deeply. "I told Colin you would come around. I told him you still loved me."

"Of course I do." She began to lead the man toward the shop. More specifically, to the alley behind, as opening the shop door was against the rules and would lead to automatic execution. Hers was not the execution she wanted.

The man pointed to the shop window. "I wish I had remembered to buy you roses."

Ava smiled. "Yep, you haven't 'botany.' Get it?"

The man paused and thought. "You were always very clever, Nora. Sometimes, too clever for your own good. That's why Colin never trusted you."

She shrugged and continued moving the man toward the darkness of the alley. "As the roses say, 'thanks a bunch.'"

"I wish you and Colin would get along. I wish you would take it more seriously. Why are you telling jokes?" The man's voice caught in his throat. "Once we are over the bridge, I may not see him again, you know? I am choosing you, choosing to be with you. I wish you would appreciate that."

"I do appreciate that." She was getting him closer to the shadows of the alley; she was seeing only green traffic lights in her mind. There was no one around, no reason to see any red with the exception of the band the man she was escorting was wearing.

"God destroyed the bridge, we didn't." His eyes began to water, and she felt as if she were carrying more of his weight. She wondered if she would have the nerve to go through with it. She knew the penalty for killing a Red Band was worse than execution. She looked in all directions again. They were alone. She knew the alley well enough to know where the cameras' blind spots were.

"Let's sit." She patted his arm tenderly as she slowly lowered herself to the ground. With her arm threaded through his, he had no choice but to sink beside her. They were leaning against the dumpster, using it for cover. Ava had also placed them on the large plastic mat that was meant to catch the clippings that came loose when she dumped out her bins. She would be able to roll the plastic into a funnel and pour the secret ingredient into her mulch bags. She would then put the body beneath the compost in the dumpster. No one checked for bodies too carefully on the day following Solstice executions.

"Nora, when you post the new message, put it on the background with the person yelling through a megaphone. The others have been told to look for that."

Ava remembered the old messages that she would smirk at while scrolling when work was slow. The images and the messages had a comical incongruence. At the time, she hadn't realized that they were secret codes, that the Red Bands were speaking to each other directly and blatantly in plain sight. She had considered the Red Bands feeble with their confused posts; she later realized that they were tacticians.

The old man wiped his eyes and sniffed. He was so fragile, so vulnerable; it was difficult to imagine that she and the others had to run from these people. It was difficult to imagine that someone like him could harm anyone at all.

Her free hand moved to her pocket where she placed it over her pruner.

"God destroyed the bridge, but it gave us the opportunity we needed. Nora, you were right about taking action, about making a move in a time of complete chaos. And you were right about them tasting so good."

Any sympathy Ava had for the man left at that moment. She struck quickly, dragging the blades across his throat. He didn't struggle as she had expected. He slumped over, shocked.

His breath came in ragged bursts and his hand spasmed along his side. At first Ava thought he was going to try to reach for her. Instead, he struggled with his pocket. Eventually, he was able to remove a small bag of pills that he handed to Ava.

"Give these to Colin, Nora. He is going to need more...to stay safe."

Ava took the pills and put them in her pocket. She turned the man on his side, allowing the blood to pool beneath him. There was a lot of blood, but less than she had anticipated.

"That should be enough," she muttered, rolling the man onto his back so that she could lift him into the dumpster. In her arms he resembled a child; they were a blasphemous Pietà. He sank into the compost as if sinking into a soft mattress. She pushed down, pushing him farther into the muck and piling more and more on top of him. She gave the dumpster a shove and could not hear or feel anything beyond the compost. Ava smiled, thinking it was almost as if the man had been swallowed whole and how fitting an end that was for a Red Band.

The roses accepted the offering of the Red Band blood, but it quickly had a detrimental effect. There was wilting. There were cankers on the canes. There were spots on the petals highlighted by reddish halos that mimicked the color of the band of the man she had murdered. In the end, she had to sacrifice a few of her bushes, and it took Herculean efforts to salvage the rest.

Ava remembered that the man had been suffering from dementia. She wondered if that condition had affected her flowers. She considered this as she examined the resurrected buds, the ones that "rose from the dead."

Two Solstices Prior

After the announcement to leave the residences was made, Ava swallowed one of the pills that had been meant for Colin. She gasped as she watched herself become translucent and then finally disappear. She laughed at herself in the mirror, her clothes and her hair elastic were the only visible aspects of her. She discarded those items, thanked the man she had killed, and took to the streets, looking for a supplier for her flowers. She did have to carry a few supplies with her, but she managed to leave them on the ground, subtly kicking them forward as she moved as if they were driven by the wind. There was no need to hide this time, no need to creep in the shadows. She walked down the center of the streets, feeling more powerful than she had in a long time. Maybe than she ever had.

It took time to find anyone. She wondered how the Red Bands guaranteed a successful hunt. No hiding was allowed, but people had become adept at remaining on the move. Ava had always resented that aspect of the Solstice. She was not naturally active. She liked to consider herself "deeply rooted," like her flowers.

She heard a cough. That sound was unusual, especially on a night when most were trying to not be discovered. She saw a woman moving stealthily along the tall hedges near the Blue Band living quarters. As Ava grew closer to the woman, she saw that she wore a red band.

This was exactly what she did not want to happen. She wanted to find a supplier that would look like a victim of the Solstice. She was not acting as a vigilante; she was only thinking of her flowers.

She wasn't sure she would find anyone else at this point, or without witnesses. The woman was completely unaware of Ava's approach as she was consumed with finding nourishment. Even though she was invisible, Ava crept up behind the woman and put a hand over the woman's mouth. The woman was small and light, and Ava had no difficulty pulling her into the hedges where her work would not be spotted.

Ava slid her supply bag toward her, removed the pruners, and pulled them across the woman's throat. She quickly placed a bag over the opening. There was a noise like a soft rain fall as the warm blood filled the bag. Ava was able to secure five bags before the blood flow dwindled.

The plants accepted the offering and seemed to flourish for a few days after. Then, the spots and cankers appeared again, lighter and smaller this time, but visible all the same.

"The Red Bands are sick," Ava said aloud, alone in the shop. The post-Solstice purchases had happened when the flowers were showing no signs of disease. What if some of the Red Bands had taken flowers home with them instead of offering them all as a tribute? What would happen to her and her business if they suspected her merchandise was damaged?

Furthermore, what did it mean that the Red Band blood was behind the flowers' disease? The first Red Band had shown signs of deterioration, but the second one had not. Were they all carriers?

By the time of the next Solstice, her other plants had begun to show effects, even though they had not been recipients of the secret ingredient. Whatever contaminant was present, it was an airborne contagion. Non-Red blood donations offset some of the damage, and Ava began targeting donors that were not allowed Solidox. Her neighbor had almost gone willingly, and for that, Ava had been grateful.

The Current Solstice

Banking on Rodeo being empty, and confident her invisibility would protect from all detection save motion sensors, Ava set out to steal some Solidox. She had to leave her supply bag outside the development, as it was sure to trigger some alarm or sensor, but she didn't need her pruner with her. She was not after fertilizer this time; she was after answers. She fancied herself an armchair chemist, and she certainly knew what compounds had positive or negative effects on her plants. If she could obtain even one pill, she could find a way to break it down—even if it meant rekindling with the phlebotomist, if he were still alive.

She didn't know where to begin once she was behind Rodeo's walls. No non-resident had ever been inside with the exception of the construction crew. She knew the homes would be locked and alarmed. While the living quarters of the other hues were identical, the houses in Rodeo were all distinct with the exception of being laden with items recovered from Solstice victims. Some of the homes were tall and baroque, others were ranch-style with ornately decorated exterior tiles. There were fountains and gazebos and driveways paved with colorful resin. There was also one house that was lit as if someone were home.

She walked around the back to get a better look. Either this resident had already eaten for the evening, or they were abstaining, which was unheard of. She peeked in a window and could see no one. The lights may have been a decoy, or they may have accidentally been left on. What was not a smokescreen was the large amount of medicine bottles that were visible from where she stood.

"The treasure trove," Ava breathed. She began to realize that she could serve a purpose beyond her plants. What if she secured enough Solidox so that the Red Bands had to go without? Better yet, what if others took the Solidox and became weaponized against the Red Bands?

Her stomach knotted at that latter thought, but taking a pile of pills off the market might be a worthwhile venture. If nothing else, it would provide her with plenty of samples to test out the issue with her roses.

She turned the doorknob slowly and found that it was unlocked. If she could move silently enough to match her invisibility, she would have a chance. She looked for a bag or sack to take the pills, knowing she would have to hide as there would be no way to make the Solidox invisible. She was proud of her soundless rummaging, until a dart found its way into her back.

She had no way to mask the thump her body made when she hit the floor. Moments later, Dr. John appeared above her. He was smiling and seemed to be looking directly into her eyes.

"I have been alone enough to recognize when I am not," he explained. He took a bottle from his back pocket and poured it over her. It was Methylene Blue and it stained her skin, working against the invisibility pill.

At least it wasn't yellow, she thought, then chastised herself for not being more concerned about her predicament. She wasn't scared because Dr. John did not have an aggressive posture. For all she knew, he hadn't taken a Solidox that evening. Plus, he was petting her.

Ava took a deep breath, her blue chest rising and falling. Dr. John was looking at her, but he didn't seem to really see her. "It just keeps getting worse. And it's spreading fast now. Even people who have not had the Solidox... They are experiencing changes."

Ava was powerless to speak or move. She was a captive audience for the ramblings of an old man. If she had learned anything from movies, it was always to let the villain speak. They gave away a lot of secrets when they were allowed a soliloquy, and it gave the hero the time to think of an escape plan.

"It's not just dementia. This is a new strain." He sighed and paused his petting. "It's like the aging we had stopped is catching up at full force."

Ava closed her eyes. She had to force herself to think. She wondered how long it took for the darts to wear off. No one had lived through it to tell the tale.

"The sickness will get everyone now. All the bands." Dr. John turned her face toward his, caressing her cheeks. "And it's my fault. That is hard to live with."

He was silent for a long time, petting her and occasionally glancing at her chest. His glances were not lascivious; it appeared that he was monitoring her breathing. "I think it might be my time soon, Miranda. Can you give me a goodnight kiss?"

Ava held her breath as Dr. John repeated, "Goodnight kiss." The last thing she wanted was a kiss, but she was powerless to prevent it. He took her face in his hands and kissed her tenderly. He then placed a pillow beneath her and went to his stockpile of medicines. He opened a drawer and removed a syringe. Ava held her breath, expecting him to inject her with something to make her even more edible. Instead, he took the needle and went into another room.

The dart wore off slowly. Ava felt pins and needles in her feet and hands first. This was followed by a burning sensation, then a hollowness in her arms and legs. It felt as if her body were far away and she was barely able to manage getting to her feet, let alone leave Rodeo.

She stepped outside but nothing looked familiar. She couldn't remember how she got here, nor could she remember where she was supposed to be.

Her body carried her home without any contribution from her mind. The streets were unfamiliar, the homes foreign. A part of her knew there was a reason for her confusion. Something had happened to her that she desperately needed to remember, something that would not only help her, but others like her.

Her feet led her into the apartment that had numerous rose bushes in the yard. She knew she should remember something about the flowers, something important. She stroked the flowers and took in their scent. They pleased her and made her feel at home, even though she could no longer remember home.

"Those are pretty," she said, looking at each bush in turn. "Except the yellow ones. For some reason, I don't like those."

Chapter 8
Sundowning

April 3

Colin became angry with me when I asked him where Nora was. He used words like "abandoned" and "gold digger," but I don't remember her like that.

I know Colin resents having to come visit me. He doesn't enjoy having to spend time with me or having to take me out. Back in the old days, he used to have to cross the bridge to get here, and the traffic was always bumper-to-bumper. Once he was here, we would have to run errands so I could get the things I needed. Then he had to return before curfew, which he lambasted every trip. He somehow blamed Nora for all the inconveniences. He has even found reason to blame her for the way the world is now. I try to explain that she has a servant's heart and puts her community first. He accuses me of seeing what I want to see. It's an argument that goes round and round, and sometimes I forget the point I am trying to make, and sometimes he storms off without even saying goodbye. He lacks patience, which is understandable. I wish I could be more self-sufficient. I miss being able to do what I want when I want. But that is the price one pays to continue living.

I can still get Solidox here in the center, but I don't always remember to take it. Colin told me I can program my phone to remind me, but I never can remember where I placed the thing. He doesn't like me taking Solidox. He thinks it is a cult, that I am part of a cult. He doesn't know what we eat when we take the medication. If he did, he would no longer allow me to take it. He would tell the nurses to keep it from me. Only the people on Solidox know what we do to feel better. We communicate with each other in ways that only we understand. I can imagine it would be disturbing or even frightening to imagine us devouring helpless cats. It is easy to judge when you are not faced with desperation. We started taking the Solidox to feel better, to stop the pain, to assuage the fear. I only take it because I hope it will help me retain the mental capacity I still have.

I hope this journal will help too. It is good for me to write down memories. It will also help me to go back and read about them if I have forgotten them. A person who visited the center told me that journaling will help me to orient myself and to deal with my feelings. What I want to write about most is the experiences of the past several years. I want to write about how the Solstices came to be. I hope that Colin will maybe read this one day and understand the choices that were made.

It started with some community changes. Back when I was in politics, we considered ourselves stewards of the people. We sought out the best ways to handle community property and we upheld laws that allowed for peaceful coexistence. The island was growing contentious, there were populations that were at odds with each other, and the strife was harming tourism. Those of us in charge had to keep a focus on the greater good. We had to help drive business to the local economy, to the privately owned businesses, we had to invest in our own people. We presented at the clubs, and we posted on social media, and we were able to gain a foothold among voters.

Then things began to change once we were introduced to the Solidox. I hadn't started taking the Solidox until after I began to lose my memory. Dr. John said that the pills could ward off aging and even reverse some of the complications of growing old. Unfortunately, Solidox was not capable of defeating an enemy that already had control over major organs.

Dr. John kindly explained what was happening to my brain. He talked of cognitive decline and what might attribute to it. He is always incredibly sympathetic when we meet; he says that many of his patients have a fear of Alzheimer's and related dementias and that he is dedicating his time to work on a medication for that. I respect Dr. John's intellect and enthusiasm. If anyone can help us, Dr. John can.

But the brain is complicated, and Dr. John knows that. I imagine he has also learned how complicated the heart can be. I am sure he is nursing his heart now that he has experienced what it is like to be loved by Nora. I had great success as a politician, but that is one campaign that no one can win. It's not that she is a formidable debater, or even an expert strategist. What she is is conniving. She is crafty and shrewd in ways I have never seen. Years ago, I had a fish finder on my boat; Nora has an internal fish finder. She always knows where to be and who to be with in order to profit the most. She always walks away with the biggest catch.

April 9

The island community has greatly changed in the last few years. The demographics now skew older and most resources are directed to this population. If I were younger, I would resent it. As a man of a certain age, I am proud to see my peers remaining active. There is a great deal of passion remaining in the old bones on the island and that is inspiring to witness. It is all thanks to the Solidox.

It wasn't harmful at first, taking those pills. The hunger was a bit concerning, but we learned how to manage that. I hate to pat ourselves on the back, but we really helped the environment. There had been a rash of feral cats; an infestation that is common on islands. Once you have two or three wild animals, they begin to reproduce. Cats reproduce rapidly. I had read once that one female cat could be responsible for 400,000 additional felines in only seven years if her offspring are all fertile. That is just one cat.

The decline in the feral population was good for community morale. It is distressing seeing cats coming to your porch to beg, their famine visible. We alleviated that problem. Eventually some pets began disappearing, but coyotes were a good source of blame. Nora came up with the idea to blame the coyotes.

The animal shelters praised the elders of the community for actively adopting, especially being willing to take in senior animals or those with disabilities. Usually adopters want kittens, but those small puffs of fur did not suit our needs. We took the ones that they thought would stay in cages indefinitely. At least we got them out of the cages.

I remember the news did a fluff piece on the pairing of elder citizens with elder felines. All that did was force a few people to have to purchase toys and cat beds and litter boxes that would never be used after the cameras went away. That newscaster, Claudia Shephard, followed up at the center to see if we had any resident felines here. She said something about "emotional support animals." I could hear her talking to the head nurse about studies showing that cats are responsive to those in hospice care. The cats supposedly ease the patients to the other side. Her sanctimonious tone made me angry. She would grow old someday too, and she would not speak of it so callously when it became her reality.

April 12

It's hard to explain how we moved on from the cats. Nora acted as our spokesperson; she spreads ideas through town and those stories became more appealing than the truth. She was the one that had convinced us to return to a cash-only policy and to focus on the well-being of the younger generation by imposing work bans so they could focus on education and their social lives. She had even persuaded me to sign off on curfews and permits to enter the island. Nora could be exceedingly persuasive when she put her mind to it. I have to admit, the overall effect of the policies she instituted was positive. In fact, it was downright quaint, so I trusted her to know what was best for our community. She was putting our safety and survival first.

And I had trusted her with our divorce. She had provided me with papers, which I signed, but there were no lawyers present. Colin had been furious about this, but I wanted what was best for Nora. She was a vibrant woman who should not be shackled to a man who was losing his mind. By the time I had entered the center, she was already remarried, and I was happy for her. He had been a judge. Something happened to him though. I don't remember what, but Nora told me he had passed, and she was heartbroken about it. She had brought me some stew she had made and that was when she told me about the judge.

April 18

I had been writing about how we moved on from cats, but I became sidetracked. That happens often now.

After I had eaten the stew, Nora told me the origin of the meat it had contained. She asked me how I felt after I had eaten it. Once I got over the shock of her confession, I realized that I was feeling better than I had in years. She told me I could continue feeling that way, that I might even see improvement. I truly believed that she would never be able to convince me, but she had a golden tongue.

We started by testing the waters. We posted on the neighborhood group and social media pages using our signature style. Most messages were in all caps. Ellipses were inserted randomly. Personal information that should never be shared publicly was provided. "LOL" meant lots of love. Our refusal to adhere to social media conventions reduced the number of likes we received until the algorithm only shared our messages with the chosen few.

We incorporated codes. We listed Bingo on the 11th or Keno on the 23rd, with both located on 64th street. We knew 11/23/64 was ingrained in the psyches of those we were trying to reach and completely disregarded by those that came after.

While it was easy for us to gather, it was not easy to convince ourselves of what we needed to do to stay healthy. It was an abomination. It was a sin. It was about as evil as things could be.

But Nora has a way. She finds a way of making you believe that everything she is saying is true. She has a way of making you feel blameless, of convincing you that your needs are of premier importance. She has a way of knowing everyone's professional history and when decisions had been made that caused for sleepless nights.

She reminded us of what we had done for the feral cat population, of the necessity of culling the herd. She asked us to consider the ethics of allowing others to suffer from pain or neglect.

It was easy to only half-agree with her when not under the influence of Solidox. When the hunger hit, ethics were effortlessly abandoned.

The children had been easy prey. Maybe even easier than the cats, as they often did not fight back. They were lured into Rodeo with promises of treats and play time in the pools. Nora did the majority of the luring. The treats were laden with sedatives.

But the children had been missed. That was why Nora convinced everyone to offer the parents shelter from the storm. It was the humane thing to do.

She had signed me out of the center so that I could visit Rodeo. She had showed me the pool and explained that they had no choice. She said that the sacrifices those people made would not go to waste. I wasn't sure what this meant, but I always trust what Nora says. She always knows what is best.

April 22

In my defense, I had messaged the mainland prior to the storm. I told officials they should come to the island. The storm was headed their way and we were outside the cone. I also convinced Colin to stay on the island in my old home. This was not exactly a mistake, as the worst of the storm was off island. The mainland was completely decimated, and word is that nearly everyone across several states was killed. We were not in the free and clear, though, and the storm hovered over us for at least a dozen hours. There was fear of a storm surge and of lives lost, but the sound of the wind was the worst part. I kept thinking of the story of the Three Little Pigs and how the wolf had huffed and puffed on the very structure of their homes. I can imagine that the smell of the wolf's breath was probably bad, but the sound of the expelled air pushing against the frames of the houses repeatedly must have been terrifying. Each gust would cause an additional crack, sounding like bones breaking. And that was what wind, and wolf's breath, does—it breaks the very bones of your shelter.

No one was on Solidox during the storm. We had all stashed some away, but there was no point in dealing with that hunger when there was no way to secure food. All animals were either burrowed underground or they had the sixth sense to evacuate early. Evacuation meant death in this case, and we feared that after the storm, our food supply would be low.

April 25

The bridge had been decommissioned after the storm. Those on the island had been assured that the Salvation Army and FEMA would bring supplies, that they would find ways to get them to us. I am not proud to write that supplies had never been requested. Those in charge did not believe that there was anyone remaining to provide them. Those in charge also saw this as the opportunity they had been waiting for.

The problem is that with no bridge, we truly weren't receiving supplies. Once the stores were emptied, that would be it. Luckily, it would take time for that happen and there might be a way to establish trade again if there were anyone to trade with.

Nora also reminded us that if it were possible to continue growing roses, then crops could also be grown. Whatever animals survived could be bred as livestock. Those animals and crops could feed people, and those people in turn could feed...

There was no power and no internet. Luckily, our group knew how to communicate without power. We requested songs on the radio, we called in to talk shows. We requested the Simon and Garfunkel song "Bridge Over Troubled Waters." We told the talk show hosts that we wanted to talk about basement renovations, even though no houses on the island had basements. Those that heard the song or heard the basement chatter knew that the rules were about to change.

Nora had been instrumental in finding shelter for those who had lost their homes in the storm. She had commandeered a school, a warehouse, a church, and other community structures that were still standing. It had been her suggestion to place people where they would feel the most comfortable. She felt that the younger people should be together so they could bond and support each other. She spoke of us being guardians for those less fortunate. She implored us to keep track of supplies and where they were going. She then led the campaign for separate living quarters for everyone. She felt it would be an easy way to keep track of the population. She said she liked to think of those of us in more fortunate positions as concierges for those who were without. It was an unusual argument, but not without its merits.

July 28

Colin visited me today. He didn't seem in a hurry as he normally did. I was glad, as I had something to give him, but he wanted to talk to me first. He sat in a chair facing me and asked, "Why did you do it? Why did you destroy the bridge?"

I know he didn't mean me personally. I was just an old man in a nursing home. I told him the truth; I told him that God destroyed the bridge. We humans just couldn't be "arsed" to rebuild it.

He argued that I made it sound like simple neglect. He said it was a strategic move to end the lives of many.

Colin wasn't wrong, but this same decision has been made over and over since the dawn of time. He should be grateful we are on the right side of the decision.

I handed him the pills I had gotten from Dr. John and had him promise me he would take them on Solstice. It was the only way I could protect him.

He, like everyone else, now knew what we had to consume when taking Solidox. He could no longer look me in the eye.

September 30

Nora came to help me for Solstice. She knew that Colin couldn't help me, nor could the Green Bands that are forced to work in the center. I am grateful she came. I would have forgotten it was Solstice and the nurses would not have bothered to remind me for their own good.

I had forgotten what Rodeo looked like. At first, it appears opulent. Upon closer inspection, it's clear that it is piled full of items that have been hoarded. It is a dump of the spoils of a one-sided war. This wasn't the intention for either Rodeo or the new rules. Everything just snowballed. I truly do not understand how we got to this point.

Nora took me to a building that had large tubes containing people, many I recognized. They were floating in some kind of liquid. They weren't alive, but they weren't really dead either. I was shocked to see them, but Nora told me to stop clutching my pearls. She said this was the natural order. We couldn't depend on Solidox indefinitely. She asked me if I wanted to stay there in the building instead of in the center. I didn't understand what she meant. If I stay there, I think I have to be in that undead position like the people in the tubes.

I had pointed to one of the tubes. It contained Shirley Watson. Shirley looked like she had been pressed in a scrapbook: her make-up was dark and smudged and her hair was tangled like seaweed in the liquid. Shirley had always been a favorite at Bingo nights. She told raucous jokes and could drink anyone there under the table. She was also an admirable dancer, very light on her feet. I used to enjoy dancing with her until it made Nora angry.

"There's Shirl," I said, and a smile must have come to my face, as Nora's eyes grew cold and she told me I looked like a fool. She walked to Shirley's tube and pulled the plug from the wall. The liquid stopped moving and Shirley's body fell to the bottom with a crash.

I was stunned and told Nora to plug it back in immediately.

"What?" she asked innocently. "We need the room. Besides, I want to plug this in." Nora smiled mischievously as she plugged her radio into the socket that had housed Shirley's lifeline. She turned the volume up so I could hear the song. It was something about moments being precious and few.

"You like this song, right?" Nora had asked me. She swayed to the music as she walked to me. She put her hands on my waist and put her arms around my neck.

I did like the song, but I was very confused about what was happening. Nora again asked if I wanted to stay in the room with "the rest of my friends." I was having a hard time remembering how this place would be different from where I currently lived. I told her I had to think about it. I also asked her for a kiss.

Chapter 9
Same Difference

"Good afternoon, my name is Claudia Shephard, and this is WBNZ News."

Claudia had her curly hair tightly secured in a top bun. The Red Bands would write letters to the station claiming they preferred her hair this way. It was *more professional.* She wore a deep-blue dress that matched the blue tie Sean was wearing with his gray suit and the blue bands they both wore around their necks. Claudia was to have enough blue dresses that she would not repeat any in a given month. Cleavage was verboten, but length did not matter as the camera never caught her legs below mid-thigh. Her mic-pack was often strapped to her calf so that she could walk with it and it would not be noticeable when she turned toward the green screen. In Chicago, it had been strapped to her waist, but in Chicago she had mostly sat at the anchor's desk. Sean was clean shaven, as was the Red Bands' preference.

Claudia read from the teleprompter:

"Due to the earlier sunsets, Daryl's will begin offering dinner at 3pm."

In Chicago, they had reported crime, politics, and entertainment. This was how she had imagined a newscaster's job to be when she had been studying communications. The new normal had changed their roles, both professionally and personally.

Sean read his portion:

"The Lavender living quarters have been placed on temporary warning. The grounds look negligent, and the window dressings are far from coordinated. A lack of pride in one's home affects us all."

They were both aware of who wrote the news they read. There was a primary author; that title was more appropriate than reporter, as the "news" was subjective and highly censored. Other sources occasionally submitted information, but those segments were heavily screened.

"And please remember to lower your headlights when entering Rodeo. The glare is disturbing to those who are trying to rest or watch television."

Claudia stood to move to the green screen. The new broadcast rules were only two newscasters per shift. They would serve as anchors, meteorologists, and special commentators upon request. Sean always made Claudia report the weather; it was her penance.

She always wondered what would happen if she lied about the weather. She was tempted to say it was going to be a gorgeous sunny day so that the Red Bands got soaked during golf or riding around in their carts or walking on the beach. It would be a mild form of rebellion, but one that would probably get her killed.

If they could prove she was lying.

She reported what she knew to be correct about the weather. She was not an official meteorologist, but she had adopted some level of skill for seeking patterns by looking at old forecasting models. The island no longer had access to satellites and radar; she had to use less scientific methods such as barometers and "red sky at night, sailors' delight; red sky in morning, sailors seek warning." Her consistency was not that far off from those who had used the Dopplers. Her biggest weather error had been that she had been wrong about the hurricane.

She hadn't reported the weather then; they had an official weather girl at that time. When the bridge was open, the station had an employee list with envious depth. She and Sean were among the few that were island residents and the audience appreciated having "some of their own" on their televisions. No one had predicted a Category 5 hurricane coming, but Sean had wanted to evacuate ahead of time.

"The station needs someone on air," she had protested, not because she felt a duty to her job, but because facing a hurricane was less painful that staying with his family off the island.

"There won't be *air*. The power will knock out right away."

"They will still have us on the radio stations though. People will still be able to hear us; they will need to be able to hear us."

"I should go without you," he had threatened. She had insisted he go, but he hadn't. He had been asking her to go with him to his parents' house for weeks. She had seen the messages on his phone, had seen his conversations with the city station for an interview to become their head anchor. It had taken her years to convince him to leave Chicago, to come with her to the paradise she had always dreamt of. There was no way she was giving up what she had fought so hard to obtain. She would give up Sean before she would ever give up the island.

Even now, even in the new normal, she had no regrets. She and Sean were safe, safer than most. The pendulum always swings back the other way. The island would be rebuilt, and the Red Bands would not be able to maintain control forever. She had faith that everything would return back to the way it was.

Golf scores were always presented last, per Red Band preference. Sean read them with gusto, knowing they were the *piece de resistance* of the broadcast.

"Alan de Winter made a 40-footer followed by a smooth five-incher to beat his average with a very respectable 95. Matthew Gates was two under on the 7th hole, which caused for a pause in the day to inspect his clubs."

In school, they had been taught to approach the news segments as individual stories. They had to paint a picture with main characters and a conflict. They were either to provide a resolution or entice viewers to tune in later for additional information. In the new normal, the Red Bands were the main characters and the news only reported what they wanted to hear.

She could never sleep when it rained.

There was an energy to the air, as if something existed between the raindrops, like dark matter helping them to fall straight to earth. Without that something, the drops would drift off, would dance in the air until they simply evaporated. The invisible matter allowed them to congregate on the ground and to become something bigger than themselves. As a child, she would thank that invisible something for allowing her to splash in the puddles, to water flowers from the bucket she kept outside, to have a reason to wear her poncho that was covered with fluorescent stars. As an adult, she knew there was nothing to thank.

She controlled her destiny and what she wanted was to be like the raindrops, to be a part of something bigger than herself. She had gone into broadcasting out of vanity. She liked being filmed, she liked people watching her. She no longer enjoyed that and would rather be a nameless face in the crowd if that meant she could be a part of something important. And nothing was more important than toppling the Red Band laws.

Sean approached her as she sat beneath the extended eave, knees drawn to her chest, arms clasped not because she was chilled, but because her arms always seemed to be folded around her like a shield lately.

"I love to sit here in the rain. It makes me feel like I am getting away with something. Not a single drop has landed on me."

"It's like you are in the catbird seat."

She eyed him beneath a long curl that had fallen in front her eyes. "What does that mean?"

"It's just a saying. It means to be in a good spot; to have the upper hand."

She pulled the neck of her sweater up over her chin. This was a nervous habit from childhood. "Which, for us, means just being alive."

Sean crouched beside her and rubbed her shoulder. "I think the saying is more complicated than that."

She snorted and the curl bounced on the pressured breath. "You can just say it, Sean. You think I have the upper hand in our relationship. Because we are here."

"I wasn't going to go there." He stiffened. She knew he was tired, physically and mentally. She did not have to square up for a fight, but that seemed to be her habit as of late.

"I just want things to be normal again. But they can't. They can't ever be normal. We've lost too much."

She knew he was talking about his family. He was alone now. Even if they were somehow able to get off the island, he would still be alone. She understood that and it made her feel impotent and she hated feeling that way. He didn't view her as family, not when he blamed her for their surviving while so many he loved did not.

"We have more than a lot of people..."

He rubbed his forehead. "For fuck's sake, Claudia, can you ever just listen without trying to change my mind? Sometimes I just need you to listen."

A part of her wanted to apologize to Sean. A part of her recognized that he was right. He had come out to check on her, to try to share his feelings with her. Instead of using this moment to strengthen their relationship, she sermonized.

He stood. "You going to come to bed?"

"Eventually. Or I might not."

"Either way," he said, and turned to climb the stairs leading into the space they shared.

Claudia felt a prickly anger over Sean's accusation. She did listen to him. She just grew tired of hearing about how she had sabotaged their chance for escape. When she would remind him that they would be dead if they had left the island, he would say that that was better than the way they were living. He said that death and their constant state of being threatened with dying was the "same difference."

She had come outside to gather her thoughts. The Solstice was soon, and she was afraid. She knew she had less to fear than others, but she was afraid nonetheless. Their status as newscasters put them in a special position. There had been times when the Red Bands recognized them during the hunt and left them alone. They could not count on that luck holding out. There may come a time when the hunger drove the Red Bands to decide that their favorite newscasters could be replaced.

Claudia wore a blue dress accompanied by sneakers. She and Sean would not have time to change in between the broadcast and the orders to assemble outside. They sat in the make-up chairs, patiently enduring the accidental pokes by their make-up artist who was already shaking in anticipation of what lay ahead.

"I have something." Claudia dug into a bag while Sean accepted his face powder. She pulled out a mask and a bandana. She had spied them in a dumpster outside Rodeo. It was against the rules to take anything from Rodeo, even the garbage, but this was something she could not resist. As a child, her favorite toy had been an old Halloween mask fashioned to look like Frankenstein's monster. She had worn it to play dates, alone in her room, every opportunity she had until the mask finally split into pieces. She had never felt braver than when that mask was the face she showed to the world. This mask wasn't nearly as ugly and therefore not as powerful. It was a nondescript piece of plastic, just two eye holes ringed with blue make-up, streaks of blush where the cheeks would be, and large pink lips pursed in a mini smile. While everyone thought that Claudia's fame was her shield, she felt that the anonymity of the mask offered some sort of protection, like being a faceless part of something larger. Behind the mask, she could do things that would never be attributed to Claudia Shepherd. That was an exciting prospect on Solstice.

"We can be in disguise," she told Sean.

"Why?" he scoffed. "It's not a party."

"I think I want to. I think I want to wear the mask."

He shrugged. "I just follow suit. I just follow you around like a puppy dog and do whatever you want to do. I followed you here, to this market, and I will follow you out there into that Hell."

She sighed. "When we first moved here, you liked it. Stop pretending like you never liked it."

He closed his eyes as the woman doing his make-up blended it across his forehead. "Who could like anything anymore?"

"Your misery is inside you, Sean. You are hurting, you are grieving, and you are not dealing with it. In all fairness, you don't have the ability to deal with it right now. But that feeling, that deep pain would follow you wherever you go. I am not going to co-sign the blame for this...world full of shit."

The make-up woman put down her tools and headed to the coffee pot. They both knew this was a ruse. Every Solstice they fought and every Solstice those around them became frustrated. They were viewed as "golden," as safe. It seemed a bit tone deaf to others for the beloved newscasters to complain.

She lowered her voice, "You took this job because you wanted it. And now it keeps you alive. It keeps us alive. They trust us, they trust our faces to deliver the news."

He scoffed. "It's not the news, it's what they want to hear."

"Same difference."

"We used to report the news. We used to have important jobs. Now we are dancing monkeys."

"Monkeys, puppy dogs, you are really feeling sorry for yourself right now. It's a bad look when all of them..." she gestured to the windows, "are about to put themselves on the line."

"Maybe you're right, maybe the disguise is the best idea. Let's put ourselves on the line too. Let's end this."

They sat in silence for a few minutes until she said, "You know, I wasn't happy back in Chicago."

He pulled the make-up towel loose from his neck and finished buttoning his shirt. "It doesn't matter. The place is burned to the ground. Gone. All of it. And all of them." As he went to take his seat at the desk, she tucked the mask into her tights.

After they provided the news, Sean read the rules. Neither of them needed a script for this part.

"You are to go outside. Do not lock your doors behind you in case an inspection is warranted. Your bands must be visible at all times. You must stay outside until the end of Solstice. Anyone returning home with be executed on sight. Following Solstice, survivors will be notified of loss of kin."

Once the evacuation order was given, the studio went dark, and all network employees exited by the fire escape stairs. The elevators were still in operation, but they had always used the stairs. It suited the sense of emergency.

The night was dark, and they moved quickly. Claudia felt as if she had to keep slowing down for Sean to keep up. Perhaps this was his chance to sabotage her. At one point she had to turn around to find him.

"Still following you like a puppy," he said.

"Well, don't. Either keep up with me or..."

"Or what?"

"Or we go it alone."

He gave a bitter chuckle. "That is what you want, isn't it? God, I wish you had had the nerve to tell me that earlier. I wish you had been brave enough to tell me how you really felt before the storm."

"So you could have left the island to die?"

"Is this really living? But hey, you get what you want, Claudia. You always get what you want. Let's split up here. I'll meet you back at our place tomorrow, or I won't."

She watched him walk away feeling a sense of relief. It would be easier to only have to look out for herself. She had grown to resent his helpless attitude and energy. She had been honest when she said she knew he could not work on his grief while also trying to survive, but his grief had become a burden for her too. She wanted to fight back, and he simply wanted to waste away. Their goals had never been perfectly aligned, but now they were incompatibly incongruent.

Claudia took a deep breath and slid on the mask. It had a funny smell, but she liked the feeling of transformation that it offered. What if she survived without being recognized? It would prove that she was stronger and more cunning than she had ever believed.

She backed up and was surprised to feel something solid behind her.

She felt disappointment instead of fear. "I didn't think you were going to literally follow me around." When she turned around, no one was there, yet she smelled cologne. She reached toward the scent and found herself touching a man's chest.

"Who?" she breathed.

"Why are you wearing that mask? Your face is what saves you."

"Why can't I see you?" She realized she was still touching him. She was proving to herself she wasn't hallucinating.

"I am protected."

"That's impossible, no one is protected."

"There is a lot you don't know. You read what they tell you to read, and they only give you approved information. Because you are safe, the rest of us don't confide in you."

She pulled her hand back as if slapped. "Did you come to find me just to antagonize me?"

There were a few minutes of silence, and she wasn't sure if he was still there until he said, "No. I wanted to find you because I have some information that is important. It needs to be heard, but I don't know how to do that."

She started moving again; standing still was a death sentence on Solstice. She hoped he would remain with her. "You just said that no one talks to me. So why tell me?"

"Because we all have to listen to you. You are the only outlet."

She stopped and turned in the direction of the voice. "So, what is your information?"

"They are weakening."

Her heart began to beat faster. This was what she had been wanting, what she knew was coming. She hadn't expected it so soon. "Who is weakening?"

"The Red Bands. They don't want anyone to know. Solidox isn't a panacea."

"Are they...dying?"

"Some of them. Others are starting to...crumble. They are not feeling like they did, and they know that they need help, they need something more."

This sounded too good to be true. "How do I know I can trust you?"

"I will prove it to you, tomorrow, I promise."

She thought for a moment. "Even if what you are saying is true, it doesn't solve anything. There are too many of them. We can't just wait them out. We can't just keep participating in Solstices until the last one dies."

"No. But if people knew, it might spark something. At the very least it would give people hope, which is something we haven't had in a very long time."

They had stopped in front of a fountain. He instructed her, "Meet me here tomorrow. I will give you proof."

When the smell of his cologne disappeared, she removed her mask and took a deep breath. Hope felt good.

Claudia was surprised to hear the voice say hello. She had imagined she would be seeing him, literally.

She snickered. "This is overkill, it's not Solstice, you don't need to hide."

"I don't want to be associated with this. Not yet. Besides, we can't just walk into Rodeo."

He was right. Rodeo had security to protect its residents from any type of uprising. She hadn't realized that was where they were going and wondered how she would enter the facilities.

She received an answer when she saw a pill floating in the air in front of her. "I'm supposed to take that?"

He laughed, and in her mind's eye she imagined a nice smile that reached his eyes, whatever color they may be. "I was nodding at you," he explained, "but then remembered you can't see me. That should prove that the pills are harmless; I forget I am invisible."

She took the pill and examined it. "Where did you get these?"

"My father. I can't say more than that without doxing myself."

As a reporter, she took note of the fact that there was a way to trace him. For now, she was more interested in the pill. "How long will the pill last?"

"Long enough."

"I need specifics. When you wake up, are you visible again? I can't go on the air tomorrow without a face." She imagined wearing the indistinct mask to report the news and found the idea appealing.

"When you wake up, you will be able to see yourself and others will too. Specific enough?"

"I'm not accustomed to taking big leaps of faith."

She felt his hand beneath hers, lifting the pill closer to her mouth. "There's a first time for everything."

While she was not in the habit of taking unidentified pharmaceuticals from anonymous sources, she truly had little to lose. She popped the pill into her mouth and swallowed it dry. Almost immediately, she began to feel light-headed, but in a good way, like she was shedding the weight of her thoughts and anxieties. The atmosphere around her felt different. It was as if she were a part of that dark matter, a part of something larger. She was no longer just a raindrop; she was blending seamlessly into the larger body of water around her.

When she looked down and could no longer see her hands or feet, she felt powerful, like she was protected by the greatest mask of all. She could get used to the feeling.

"You have...you have to take off your clothes," the voice said.

She blushed, then realized he couldn't see her face, or any of her.

"It feels weird at first, but you will get used to it. In fact, it will feel like a real step backward in terms of freedom when you have to wear clothes again."

It was a warm night and she wondered what this man did on the Solstices when it was colder. Then she realized, if one were invisible, one could simply go back indoors. The Red Bands would never know. She was just beginning to piece together all the liberties this pill offered when they came upon a building in Rodeo.

It was a large storage area, but Claudia was not ready for what was being stored. There were figures in clear caskets with tubes feeding the bodies intravenously. The lights were dim, and they cast a greenish tint on the liquid that was suspending the bodies. Claudia thought of her Frankenstein's monster mask, which also had a green tint. Somehow that mask was less monstrous than the undead in front of her.

"They are hoping to be resurrected. Cured," the voice explained. "Dr. John started creating the chambers when he began to get sick. I'm not sure how much progress he has made or has been able to make."

"How do you know he is sick?"

"Same answer, my father."

She knew he would provide nothing more, so she went in a different direction in terms of information. "What is going into them? There is an IV or something."

"It's a blend." She could hear him swallow before he continued. "It's made from...those people...those farmers and locals that they put in the pool during the storm. They suffocated them in there. They had placed some piping in the floor and...machines. They were able to grind the bodies and pump the nutrients out."

"Your father told you all of this?"

"Not exactly. I was able to get his passwords—they really were not that difficult to guess. He had kept journals for as long as he was able. His mind...he lost a lot of the things he used to know. But even after he stopped remembering things, they kept him included in the messages being sent amongst the Red Bands. Either they forgot to remove him, or they just didn't care."

"So, these people agreed to this, to be kept in these chambers to be cured later?"

"They don't want to die."

Claudia wondered what Sean would think of this. He was cultivating a death wish, while these people were willing to roll the dice for an opportunity to live again.

"At this point, I don't think Dr. John will be able to save them."

"Doesn't matter," she said, thinking aloud. "They are completely vulnerable here. We could knock them all off at once. Destroy the bodies."

There was a pause before he answered. "The machines keeping their vitals would set off alarms. We would be found and killed."

"They would have to see us to kill us. Besides, we are already dying unless we do something."

"Believe me, I am all in favor of the idea, but I don't think it will be successful if it is just the two of us. We can raise a militia. You can get the word out. That's why I found you. If we gather a small army and then destroy these corpses, we can fight off the last of them."

"We've never been able to do that before."

"We didn't know they were sick before. We were the sick ones before, the ones *without*. We had no food, no money, we were completely broken. And most of us have nothing to fight for."

She thought about Sean. His family was gone, his opportunities were gone. All he had was Claudia, and she had been very cold to him.

"Do you have enough pills for a group of us?"

"I think so. We might not need to be invisible if we're planning to fight though. Or, at least, all of us wouldn't need to be. We sneak a few people in to dispose of these Red Bands and then we have others waiting as defense against an attack."

She believed it could work. This was also the larger movement she was so invested in becoming a part of. "Let me talk to Sean. We can try to get the word out. We can use hidden messages, just like the Red Bands did at the start of all this."

There was more silence before he said, "We might not be successful."

She shrugged, even though, like the rest of her, it could not be seen. "They say that success is simply moving on from failure."

"For us, failure means death."

She shrugged again, this time knowing she was shrugging to herself. "Failure...death... In the new normal it's all the same difference."

"First, you wanted us to run around incognito on a suicide mission. Now you want us to follow someone you have never even seen and jeopardize our careers...and lose our lives."

"Look at how you prioritize career over life," Claudia sneered. She understood Sean's point and his trepidation, but he was an easy target for her anger and frustration. She wanted him to be included in this, but she would proceed without him if necessary.

"If my career had ever been a priority, I wouldn't have come to this second-hand station with you."

"This is an opportunity to make a difference. The biggest difference."

"I don't care."

She was tired of his attitude. "What do you even care about anymore, Sean? You said it yourself; you are in this suspended state—not dead, but not really alive either."

His eyes grew sad. "I care about you. At least I did. I cared enough to put you ahead of my needs. But I never got that in return. And now it's too late."

"You keep saying that." She flopped down on the couch beside him at the same time as he stood. "You're resigned to giving up. It's not too late, Sean. We can help with this...revolt. We can help to lead it. We can put an end to the Solstices. Isn't that what you want?"

Sean paced. "How do you know this guy isn't one of them?"

"I can tell by his voice."

"Well, that's splendid. You realize this could all be a trap. They could be leading a bunch of us into their...bunker to feed their undead. There weren't that many people who went missing after the storm to feed them indefinitely."

She had thought of that, and the idea was terrifying. "I just feel like we can trust this guy. He is taking big risks—"

"Like what? You don't even know who he is."

She would never be able to convince him to trust her intuition, not after she had said it would be safe to ride out the storm.

Sean stopped pacing and looked her in the eye. "We didn't see any of the other...plans coming. This could be more of the same. Another sick twist, a new way to torture us."

She shook her head. "The Red Bands are growing scared. Don't you feel it? If we start dropping clues—"

"We mobilize them to...do worse than they are doing now." He sighed. "You are going to do whatever you want, without a thought about me."

"I want you on my side, Sean. We have always worked better as a team."

"When was that?"

"Sean..."

He sat beside her, closer than he normally did. "You have sabotaged me enough. I can't let you destroy me."

She tried to pull back, but he was aggressively close to her face. She asked, "What does that mean?"

"I might have to stop you."

"The storm is nearly over," Claudia said in front of the green screen. She didn't have to steal a glance at Sean, as he had already gotten up from his seat and stormed off to the make-up room. They had been having unusually beautiful weather for the past week, so she knew her statement would be picked up by someone. What she didn't know was how to get to the audience she was trying to reach and make them understand. She had been practicing saying her lines with an honest face in front of the mirror. She had a small tell when she lied: a dimple in the corner of her mouth. She wished she had the Frankenstein's monster mask to hide behind, but that would really make the weather suspicious. *"The clouds are lifting,"* she proclaimed before prompting a commercial break so that Sean could come back for the latest golf scores.

"Your turn," she called into the make-up room. She knew he would come out and finish the broadcast. He was a professional and he was also too afraid to go against the Red Band's wishes.

"The latest scores from the green..." he read, but the segment was shorter than usual. There were fewer players to report on, despite the weather having been perfect.

When he finished and the studio lights dimmed, she whispered, "Do you believe me now? Where were all the golfers?"

"Are you trying to say they are in some cryotherapy chamber?"

"That or they are falling too ill to play and are on their way to becoming some...living embalmed creature."

He bit his lower lip; she knew that he did this when thinking. That gave her hope that he might come around. "We can show you. I can prove it to you." She took his hand. "Sean, if you see it with your own eyes, will you help us then?"

He looked down at their hands. "You are asking me to take some drug and then follow you and a complete stranger into Rodeo?"

"Yes, that is exactly what I am asking you to do."

He bit his lip again before saying, "I just follow you around like a puppy dog..."

Claudia heard a voice from behind her as she removed her make-up in the studio.

"I have been watching your broadcasts. How is anyone supposed to know what you mean? Tonight, you mentioned an eclipse. What are viewers supposed to do with that?" There was a pause before he added, "Rumor is you are losing it."

Claudia put down her moistened wipe and looked into the mirror even though it reflected her face alone. "Is that right? Well, I have no idea what I'm supposed to do. You show me something very important and then leave me to figure it out on my own." She sighed. "Besides, I need a way to reach you beyond waiting for you to creep up on me."

"I can't give you my name yet, or where I live."

"Okay, then I'll think of something. I need a bit more time."

"Time is something we don't have a lot of."

She nodded. "I know. Listen, even though you are accusing me of being irresponsible and ineffective, I am actually glad you are here. Sean needs to see it for himself. Can you show him what you showed me? Can you give him a pill?"

The silence following her question was long enough for her to assume he had left.

"I can get him a pill. Wil you be needing another one too?"

She didn't like the antagonism in his voice. "I don't think he'll go without me. He's not as trusting as I am." She bit her tongue after saying that as she knew that Sean would argue that he trusted her too much, to his own detriment. It was that he didn't trust anyone but her, and she had proven that she didn't deserve his trust.

"Okay. You both go. Then we strategize. The objective was to get the word out."

"And beyond the broadcast, how would you like me to do that? We don't have cell phones anymore. We don't have internet. We can't march into any of their clubs, and we can't start any clubs of our own."

She was faced with more discouraging silence.

"The mask," he finally said.

"What?"

"That mask you were wearing. It can be a symbol. We can take pictures of it—I still have an old camera and can develop film. We make signs, we spray paint it, we create art in the living quarters that serve as messages."

"How will people know what the mask means?"

"Everyone knows what a mask means. It means anonymity. It means the ability to get away with actions that you would not want your face attached to. It means that you don't have to be afraid."

Claudia smiled. "It means we all have the same face; we are all one."

"If you want to think of it that way. Remember how the Red Bands used Kennedy's death as a code? We apply things that meant something to us, but that they wouldn't remember, like Harambe. We will have to have small meetings and rely on word being spread from individual to individual. The danger is, we won't be able to officially gather until it is time to take action. We won't truly know our number in advance, and our army may be small."

"A small army is still an army."

She could hear him smile. "I like the way you think. You are either very smart or very dangerous."

It was her turn to smile. "Same difference."

They had agreed to meet in the same spot, in front of the fountain, as it was close to Rodeo but far enough away to not draw suspicion.

Claudia and Sean pretended to be on a date while they waited, although there was no one around to bear witness. Eventually the man's voice was heard, and the pills were snuck into their hands. Taking one last look to make sure no one was watching, they swallowed the pills and removed their clothing as soon as they were invisible.

"This feels weird," Sean said. Claudia felt his hand brush her side and knew he was trying to hold her hand.

"You'll get used to it," she assured him, heading him in the direction of Rodeo.

"We shouldn't talk on the way. We don't want anyone to realize we are here," the man instructed.

It wasn't long before Sean broke the silence. "I don't...I don't feel so good, Claudia."

Ordinarily she could tell if he were sick by just looking at him. She was frustrated that this means for prognosis was denied. His hand was clammy in hers and she felt him pulling on her, as if stumbling while he walked.

"Do you need to sit?" she asked Sean.

"We don't have time. If he is not well, then this piece of the mission is cancelled."

"That's ridiculous," Claudia snapped. "You can stop with the marching orders. In fact, I can wait with Sean and then take him in myself." Claudia pulled on Sean's arm, lowering him to the ground. She gently felt for his head which she laid on her lap. He was sweaty and his skin pulsed with heat. As she caressed his cheeks, she felt spittle accumulating around his mouth.

"Sean?" She bent over him carefully, placing her face near his. "He's not answering."

"Please lower your voice."

"Lower my voice? He's not answering me. He's struggling." She did quiet so that the man could hear Sean gasping for breath. "What did you give him?"

"I gave him the same pill I gave you."

"Why would it have this kind of effect?"

"Is he allergic to anything?"

"Jesus Christ." She thought for a moment. "Just shellfish."

"No nut allergy or anything?"

"Are there nuts in the fucking pills?"

"I honestly don't know what is in them. I'm just trying to figure out what is going on like you are."

She wasn't sure she believed him.

"We need to get help."

"How? We take an invisible person to Dr. John?"

"Oh my god, Sean." She began patting his face, trying to stir him alert. "If only we could see him." She could feel the man kneeling at Sean's side. "What are you doing?"

"Seeing if he needs CPR."

"I don't want you touching him."

"I am trying to help. Claudia, he is not..."

"I can handle this. I can take care of him. I don't want anyone touching him." She lifted Sean's head in her arms and rocked back and forth. She was panicked. Sean was the one who was good in these situations. She needed him to come back to her and help. "I'll handle this. I'll take care of him. I am all he has."

"Claudia, listen to me, he's not..." The man tried to free Sean's head from Claudia's grasp, but she was not letting go. "Claudia, you are not helping him."

"Why is everyone against me?" She was blubbering now. She knew she had lost control. All of the emotions she had bottled up, all of the fear and disappointment and anxiety erupted. She had kept it together for so long, trying to avoid Sean's baiting about the hurricane, trying to appear composed on camera. She had no resources left to fight the storm inside her. "I love him. I have always tried to protect him." She put her head on his and realized that she no longer felt breath coming from his mouth or nose. Gasping, she moved her hands down to his neck. No pulse.

"What is happening?" she cried.

"We have to take him. We have to get out of here."

"You did this to him. You gave him something...something different from what you gave me."

"That's not true. Listen, I am going to go grab one of the golf carts. I can slip in and out without them seeing me. I need you to stay right here with him. Don't move. We'll put him in the cart and then drive him back to your place."

"And then what?" she managed to ask between sobs.

"We wait until morning. When we are visible again, you will have to make an announcement."

Claudia cradled Sean through the night. When morning broke and they were visible, she set out to make arrangements. She would say something during the broadcast. She would announce that Sean would not be returning. She needed to find the words to stress the finality of the situation, but she also did not want to put the finality into words.

The man had stayed with her, even though she hadn't needed or wanted him there. He moved about her kitchen as if he were familiar with it, making coffee for them both. "This tragedy does not need to be for nothing," he was saying, and Claudia realized that he was taller than she had pictured. A little younger too. "We can use this to mobilize our people."

She couldn't believe what she was hearing. "You're asking me to weaponize what happened to the man I love?"

He shook his head. "The very fact that he will not be on television anymore will strike a chord. You don't have to do anything. We are all so accustomed to seeing him. We were all convinced he was safe—"

"Wait, you're going to imply the Red Bands were behind his...death?" She could barely bring herself to say the word. Saying it made it more real.

"Weren't they? We wouldn't have been sneaking around if it weren't for them."

"We wouldn't have been sneaking around it if weren't for you." She buried her face in her hands, trying to stifle a sob. "What was I thinking? I don't even know who you are, and I followed you... I got Sean to follow you—"

"Colin."

"What?"

"My name. It's Colin. You know that about me. You also now know what I look like." He touched his throat. "You see my blue band so you know which living quarters I am in. What else would you like to know?"

She shook her head. There was nothing she needed to know at this point. She simply wanted to vanish. To no longer care.

"We will make a move soon," Colin said. "I'll see who I can gather." He had started for her door and then paused. "Do you still want to be included?"

She carefully considered his question. As much as she would have preferred to be numb, to isolate, to sink into grief, she felt a compulsion to see the plan through. Colin was right, Sean was a casualty of the Solstice, even though he had not been consumed. She was thankful he had not been consumed. She would participate in the uprising, only instead of using it to find self-fulfillment, she would do it for Sean.

She could never sleep when it rained. Having spent weeks seeing Sean's face on posters hadn't made it any easier to rest soundly. This night, there would be no sleep; this was the night of the attack.

The motivational messages had not used the word "attack." They had talked of uprisings, of revolts, of revolutions. For those harder to convince, terms like transformation and reform were used. But Claudia knew exactly what it was. It was carnage. And she was happy to participate.

The posters had read *Remember SEAN*. The posters had been permitted in common areas as the messages were meant to denote a shared grief. The Red Bands missed their trusted newscaster and wrote to the studio asking for an explanation behind his death. "*He was so young,*" they would write, focusing on the possibility of an undiagnosed health issue. In the Red Band world, no one committed suicide, no one overdosed, and certainly no one expired during a raid gone wrong. The Lavender and Blue Bands saw meaning in the posters. They knew that SEAN was an acronym for *Solstice Ends, Avenge Now*. It was a call to action. The Green Bands had been left in the dark as they still benefitted from the Red Bands so their inclusion was too risky.

Claudia waited outside in the rain until Colin arrived. He had already taken his pill, but the rain sketched an outline that made him visible if one knew what to look for. He tried to hand her a pill, but she refused. "I don't need a pill," she said, pulling on her mask. "Save it for someone else."

"The face of anarchy," Colin muttered, and she could tell he was studying her mode of concealment.

"Not anarchy, necessary development," she corrected.

"Same difference."

She remembered how often Sean had said those same words. He had used them to illuminate her irrationality or stubbornness. Sometimes, the words were misapplied, but often they caused her to pause and recognize a flaw in her argument. This time, the words lit a fire in her, which led her to help light the fires inside of Rodeo. The fires raged and consumed and destroyed, but they also cleansed and purified.

It was all the same difference.

Chapter 10
The Day After

"What's your favorite constellation?"

Lek was baffled. "I never thought about it. What's yours?" He was additionally baffled as they were looking at the clouds on a sunny day, yet Amber was thinking of stars.

"It's probably cliché, but Orion."

He laughed; he often found himself laughing at her. "Why is that cliché?"

"Because I feel like everyone would say that." Amber leaned close, whispering, "You have to keep an eye on his belt. The gremlins will move the stars."

He slid his hand into hers. They were with a large group of friends, yet they were two apart, just as he wanted it. He had been waiting for the right opportunity to let her know how he felt. The day following their successful uprising seemed like the opportune time, the atmosphere was decidedly hopeful. "No one can move the stars," he laughed.

"Don't be so sure of that. Life is full of surprises."

"Speaking of which." He turned toward her and cupped her chin in his hand. She did not shrug him off, but looked deeply into his eyes. His luck had been off the charts lately, as if he were protected by an unseen force. There had been something wrong with the dart that had been shot into his neck during a prior Solstice. The Red Bands had been targeting the Lavender Bands, confident there would be no fighting back after being darted and wanting to consume their youth. The Red Bands thought that the younger meat would combat the issues they were beginning to face. This switch in hunting tactics had motivated the Lavender Bands to risk joining forces. Once Operation SEAN was introduced, they had grasped on to that movement.

Lek had been darted and had fallen, but as the old man had leaned over him, Lek had begun to feel his extremities again. It had begun like pins and needles and then graduated to a burning that reminded him of the time he had been stung by a jellyfish. There had been something wrong with the dart and Lek was prepared to take full advantage of that.

The man had bitten him—a bite that had remained red and inflamed long after that Solstice. The scar was an active reminder of how he had had to beat the man to death to get him to stop. It had been self-defense, it had been necessary, but it had still felt awful.

Amber tapped his scar lightly as she put an arm over his shoulder. "What I am surprised about is that this is not healing like it should. It looks like it still hurts...it still seems raw."

He was disappointed in the change of subject, but he knew she was right. While he had been feeling lucky to escape death, he had also been feeling strangely. At times, his thoughts escaped him. He would find himself entering a room and not knowing why he had entered. He would lose parts of conversations. He had to write things down that he wanted to remember and that was unusual for him. Unusual for most his age.

He remembered when his grandmother had been diagnosed with dementia. She had been old then, older than even some of the Red Bands. It had been scary to watch her lose her faculties, and he now feared he was becoming like her.

"Anyway." Amber looked back to the sky. "That's it, the last Solstice."

Lek wasn't so sure. "We didn't get all of them. They are still out there and probably still acting as if nothing has changed."

"I bet they are running scared. We burned down half of Rodeo. Also, we are not participating. We stopped being sheep. Lord only knows how we let it happen in the first place, but we are officially done." She pulled on the lavender band that was still around her neck and visually incongruent with her words. "And I am moving out and moving on."

Lek's heart sank. "What does that mean?"

"It means I am going to see what land is still available in this mess of a world. There has to be a way to the mainland, like an abandoned boat or even a surfboard."

"What if there is nothing there? Like, there is no mainland, it's all gone?"

Amber shrugged. "There has to be *something*. And I don't care if it's burnt. You know what burnt land means?"

Lek thought about it. "Scorched earth?"

She laughed. "A fresh start. We can be pioneers." She lifted her head and gave him a quick kiss on the mouth, which both surprised and pleased him. "You want to risk it all with me, Lek? A fresh start?"

That did sound appealing. He was about to answer when a woman strolled by them slashing sparklers against the sky.

"Where did you get those, Lee?" Amber asked. It wasn't dark enough for sparklers, but the feeling of celebration supported the choice.

"Some of us raided the market last night. We figured it was ours for the taking after laying the law on Rodeo."

Amber raised her eyebrows at Lek. "See? It's a new beginning. We can start over. No more fear, no more struggling. Or, at least, the struggle will be ours."

Lek tried to remember what they had been discussing. *What had happened at Rodeo?*

She took his hand and laced her fingers through his. "So, what do you say?"

He shook his head, not because he was refusing, but because he was trying to shake the fog loose. He wanted to remember what they had been talking about, what he was being asked to agree with.

Their chat was interrupted by a scream. A woman crashed through the shrubs that surrounded the lavender living quarters. She was disheveled and wearing a shirt that read *Boat Hair; Don't Care.*

The woman fell to her knees beside a couple reclining on a blanket. She grabbed the arm of the man closest to her and sank her teeth into his bicep.

"What the fuck?!" the man screamed and tried to pry her off him. His boyfriend began beating her on her back and about her head.

Almost instantly, others sprang from the bushes, racing toward those that had been relaxing, biting any and all available flesh. The attackers were in bad shape. One man's eye dangled from its optic nerve. Another was dropping teeth as if he were scattering rose petals.

The woman in the *Boat Hair* shirt released her victim's arm and stabbed him in the neck with a dart from her purse. He fell back, his eyes still open and staring at the clouds as Lek and Amber had been doing. The woman traced one long nail down his chest. "John," she whispered, "this does not taste like goodnight kisses at all."

Lek realized that Amber was trying to pull him to his feet. "We have to run," she urged.

He looked around and saw a scene of devastation, but his mind could not make sense of it. He also could not remember the name of the woman in front of him, the one holding his hand and trying to make him move.

"I don't—" he started to explain but was interrupted by her kissing him with a strong, quick kiss.

"Lek, please, we have to go."

The word *Lek* sounded strange coming from her mouth, but he knew it was his name. He allowed her to pull him away from the crowd. He could hear screams of pain and fright. He could also hear voices asking in concern where they were and how they got there.

The *Boat Hair* lady sat back on her ankles and yelled to the sky, "This sickness. It's spreading too fast!" She began pulling at her hair, making it messier than it would have been on the windiest boat ride.

The girl holding his hand stopped abruptly and looked at him. "Wait," she said. "What are we doing?"

"I don't know," Lek answered, and it was true. He knew nothing and he was aware that this was not how things were supposed to be. Despite being mentally adrift, he found that he was no longer afraid; he lacked the agency required to be afraid.

"Don't get bitten," someone yelled. "It's the saliva. You'll get sick from their saliva."

He felt himself being pulled back down onto a blanket. He was half-lying on the blanket and half-lying on a person who was no longer moving. The person beneath him was cold and the part of his brain that kept trying to register where he was wondered why the body was cold. Then, he forgot about the body.

"What is your favorite constellation?" a woman beside him asked, and Lek wondered what a constellation was.

Chapter 11
The Change

Leroy would pay to watch a kiss. A kiss could cause *the change*, that was why the price was so high. People like him, people who were alone, were safe. He had survived the Solstices only to be faced with this new world order of quarantine and isolation.

He remembered how his father had hated change. If the man had lived to see this virus that they had named "the change," it probably would have sent him to his grave.

Leroy wanted to see a kiss as he hadn't seen one since the Solstices ended. The good news was, he wouldn't have to pay extra if the change happened: there would be no sentient being to pay.

Laoise had been sitting beneath an awning when she had seen Leroy approach. She recognized him from the market. She hadn't been in the market in a while. She hadn't been able to afford food for the past two days and medicine for even longer.

Laoise slipped on the mask she donned when begging. It was a mask that looked similar to the ones many had been wearing around the time of the uprising. The newscaster, Claudia Shephard, had begun the mask tradition. Some had taken them from stores or stolen them from homes as a way of showing unity. Laoise had found hers among some old Halloween items that she had never felt comfortable throwing away.

"Sir, money?" she asked when Leroy was in front of her. She hated having to beg, but the quarantine made work difficult to find.

He told her what he wanted and how much he was willing to pay. She knew who she would ask. Anne had been her neighbor in the lavender quarters, and they performed together from time to time for money. Their performances were sexual in nature; they had never been asked to kiss. They teamed with each other exclusively. She and Anne had kept themselves safe from the change by not coming into close contact with anyone else.

The girls who were not careful, who had let down their guards for extra money, found themselves lost. No memories, no desires, no sense of self at all. The change snuffed out the past as if it were a candle.

She promised to meet the man in an hour. She promised she would have someone she could kiss.

The girls returned in outfits they considered sexy and wearing the masks they regularly wore. Customers liked the sense of anonymity. While the girls could see the men's faces, the men could imagine any face beneath the masks. They could convince themselves they had hired the famous actress they used to have a crush on when the film industry had still been running. They could picture the sweet girl-next-door, or the ex they wanted to humiliate.

"It's something we haven't done before," Anne said shyly, facing Laoise and not looking at Leroy.

"We'll be fine, Dolly." Laoise knew the nickname would calm her friend. Anne had spoken of a kitten she had named Dolly when she was a child and Laoise had applied the moniker to her. Kittens were safe thoughts, especially now that Solidox was no longer available. Laoise placed her hand above Anne's breast and felt her racing heartbeat.

"None of that," Leroy corrected. He had paid for a kiss in a world where kisses no longer existed.

"If something happens to me," Laoise said, "she gets extra."

Anne's eyes welled with tears of both fear and sadness. "I wouldn't care. If something happened to you, I wouldn't want to live. I would feel so guilty."

"It wouldn't be your fault." Laoise pulled her mask up farther to make eye contact with Leroy. She saw a glimmer of recognition on his face and hoped this wouldn't put a damper on his ardor. "Promise. Promise she would get my share, and more."

Leroy shrugged. He already had his hand inside his long coat. It was obvious what he was doing.

"We've been careful," Laoise whispered. They leaned toward each other. Laoise could feel Anne's breath on her lips.

"Hurry," Leroy urged, his hand moving furiously behind the cloth of his coat.

Their lips met. They had performed many acts of intimacy, but they had never kissed due to the threat of the change. Anne's lips were soft. They were sweet from the scented lip gloss she wore.

Laoise's tongue parted Anne's lips momentarily before pulling away. She could hear the man grunt as he finished.

"See, Dolly? That was easy. Now we get our money and go."

Laoise did not like the look on Anne's face. There was an emptiness to her eyes. Anne looked from Laoise to Leroy and back again before crouching down as if unsure of how to move about on this earth.

"Dolly?" Laoise's voice cracked.

Anne opened her mouth, but no sound came out. She had already forgotten how to speak. Laoise looked at Leroy expectantly, as if he may be able to help put her world back together again.

Leroy pulled a wad of cash from his coat and tossed it to Laoise. "Keep the change," he said solemnly.

Acknowledgments

I would like to express my deepest gratitude to JournalStone/Trepidatio Publishing for taking on this project. In addition, I would like to extend extra appreciation to Scarlett R. Algee for all she does behind the scenes.

About the Author

Elaine Pascale, AKA "The Godmother of Horror," is the author of *The Blood Lights; If Nothing Else, Eve, We've Enjoyed the Fruit; The Kitchen Witches;* and *The Language of Crows.* She has also had stories published in over two dozen magazines and anthologies. She is the co-editor of *Dancing in the Shadows: A Tribute to Anne Rice.* She is a regular contributor to Pen of the Damned and the Ladies of Horror Picture-Prompt Challenge. She is an active member of the HWA. Elaine enjoys chocolate, a robust full moon, reading spam emails, and paddleboarding.

Find out more at:
Website: elainepascale.com
Amazon: https://www.amazon.com/author/elainepascale
Facebook: elaine.pascale
Instagram: @doclaney
TikTok @elainepascale
YouTube: https://www.youtube.com/@elainepascale/videos
Newsletter: https://elainepascale.substack.com/

www.ingramcontent.com/pod-product-compliance
Lightning Source LLC
Chambersburg PA
CBHW020704260626
47157CB00008B/3139